HOUSE OF
HOUSES

ALSO BY KEVIN L. DONIHE

HOUSE OF HOUSES

Kevin L. Donihe

ERASERHEAD PRESS
PORTLAND, OR

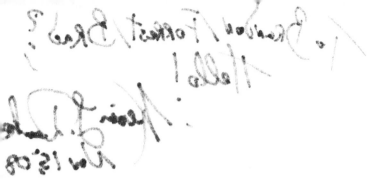

ERASERHEAD PRESS
205 NE BRYANT
PORTLAND, OR 97211

WWW.ERASERHEADPRESS.COM

ISBN: 1-933929-70-7

AUTHOR'S NOTE

Welcome to the 'House of Houses.' I hope you enjoy your stay, 'cause if you don't I'll have to gut you with deer antlers (twelve-point) torn fresh from my wall.

Love to all (or most)!

— Kevin L. Donihe
Date, '06

SECTION 1:

HOUSE HELL

CHAPTER ONE

Something is weird here. My nose is flush with the ceiling. Textured plaster digs into my bridge in a way that's neither comfortable nor uncomfortable, just perplexing. Usually, the ceiling is nowhere near my nose.

Perhaps I'm levitating. I'd done that once before, but I was five then, and that was over twenty years ago. Not certain how or why it happened. I just remember waking up to find myself floating down the hallway in my tightie whities, waving at my parents as I passed their bedroom door as if nothing was amiss.

But my arm, it's trailing off the bed, and I feel wood against my fingertips. That the bed might levitate seems logical, but not the entire floor. And something's wrong with the wood, too. The boards feel rougher, more splintery than usual, like they've cracked and buckled overnight.

The New Madrid fault cuts a groove just beyond the other side of the state, in northeastern Arkansas and southeastern Missouri. When it shook in 1812, the Mississippi River flowed backwards and church bells rang out in Philadelphia. If that thing had gone off and caused immense damage 600 miles east, then Memphis is surely a crater now, bubbling with magma and more questionable substances brought forth from the center of the Earth.

Perhaps Nashville, over 250 miles east of that city, had

likewise been destroyed. And what of Knoxville? That's even closer to home. Had the ball-tipped tower of the '82 World's Fair collapsed? Were dozens of people beneath it, dead and/or screaming? How many hearts had stopped and how many lungs were filled with blood in that town alone?

I shake away such thoughts. I'm working myself up needlessly. All I know for sure is that I perceive my nose, along with the remainder of my body, as being pressed between the ceiling and the bed. Though rendered immobile, I feel no pain. No trace of split skin or twisted bone. I dart my tongue and note the absence of bloody froth on or around my lips. Genitals, thank God, are likewise intact, though the ceiling is pressed against them in a way that's more unpleasant than hurtful.

Maybe it wasn't an earthquake. Maybe my house had been condemned without me realizing it. Sure, the place is (was?) a little cluttered, but it's a neat, orderly, if not loving clutter. Since when does that warrant a surprise wrecking ball? And how could the city-people have known, unless they had eyes in the wall, or wall-piercing surveillance via satellite? Perhaps it was an issue of Imminent Domain.

Whatever the case, I doubt the neighbors will provide assistance or dial 911. I rarely see them leave their houses, so I sometimes imagine their places are really empty and discarded sets. The papers in their boxes disappear day after day, though. Someone's getting them.

Still, even if they took the time to glance at my unfortunate house, they'd probably just call the city housing inspector, who'd hum and haw about my property before slapping a 'condemned' sticker on what used to be the front door. A contracted wrecking crew would then arrive to take down the debris, followed by a trash crew to haul it off. Not a soul would have searched for survivors.

The only neighbor (*neighbot*?) I ever see leave is one called 'Harold.' He waves whenever we're both outside at the same time, which happens about once or twice a year. He once told me—I believe last fall—that he had a skin condition that made it impossible for him to step into the sun without protective clothing and special headgear, but I think that was just an excuse for him to avoid me, too. He wasn't wearing anything on his head at the time, and all I saw on his body were shorts and a t-shirt.

Maybe I'm not giving the neighbors enough credit. They surely have emotion, if not traces of empathy somewhere in their dark and crispy souls. And I don't live in the middle of nowhere. Cars filled with people pass up and down this street, and not all of them are neighbors. Surely, they'll report something to someone.

Even if they don't, what will ultimately happen? Death? But what is death now? It doesn't mean what it used to, not when Helen lies collapsed and dying atop me, a wilting flower.

Helen—my house—is the closest thing to a wife and a lover that I've known. I thought we'd be together our entire lives. I worked at home so I'd never have to leave her, and even went so far as to move her twice, once cross country, when I felt a change of scenery might do her good.

I just wish I'd had the sense to consummate our love. I bathed in the dark, dressed in the dark, all because I wasn't ready to show her my nakedness. I needed coaxing from my shell in order to blossom into an openly sexual being, but, being a house, Helen could do little to aid my transformation.

Now, I may never transform. I don't think the reality of this has sunk in yet, but it will. I've just got to give it time, and then I'll realize how the ghosts of my upbringing have won the battle and prevented me from ever achieving true union, and thus true happiness, with Helen.

My parents insisted, for years and years, that loving nonhumans was wrong. They said the thing they worshiped—that-thing-which-may-or-may-not-be-God—would surely look upon the consummation of our love with eyes of fire.

Learning that they felt this way came as no surprise. They never treated my childhood home with respect. They didn't love it or feel its inner passageways like I did. Dishes were left in the sink for days. The floor was never swept, and months passed before newspapers were discarded. Mom worried constantly. She worried about her appearance and she worried about Pounce the cat. She worried about the weather and she worried about what she was going to cook for supper, and what she would watch on the television afterwards. Late at night, she worried that people with nebulous grudges against her were sneaking into the house when everyone was asleep to draw genitals on her Hummel figurines. Dad was distant, if not unapproachable.

Sometimes, when I'm near sleep, I'll have night terrors. I imagine I'm back at my old house, and the ghost of every burp and the spirit of every fart are trapped forever inside its walls. They taunt me and glide over my things, making them smell like old, dead farts, a smell only I can smell.

Once, I asked a teacher at my elementary school if she'd ever smelled the farts, perhaps at her place, but she just looked at me weird and, in less than a week, had me transferred to the developmental classes where I was forced to mingle with the diseased and the retarded until I left high school.

I have not and will never fart inside my house. Though I imagine that I fart less than most people, I must nevertheless fart every so often. So, when I feel wind gather inside me, I run out onto the lawn and expel gas where Helen doesn't have to smell it, or be haunted by its undying ghost.

I hate that I must defecate in her, but the neighbors started posting letters of complaint on the door whenever I shat in the yard. I always did it under the cover of night, holding matter in my bowels until it got tight and impacted, so I have no idea how they saw me, unless they were waiting for me to come out, or had cameras trained on my yard at ungodly hours.

Ultimately, I ascertained the one way to assuage both parental and *neighboral* guilt: make it legal and marry the old gal. (My house is 81 years young.) I felt reactionary thinking this way, but if that's what it took to make me feel comfortable in Helen's love, then so be it.

Two nights ago, I drilled a hole in the wall by the bed in preparation for the honeymoon scheduled to commence the moment everything had been sanctioned by—or at least brought to the attention of—a higher authority. No priests or preachers or teachers or rabbis were to perform the ceremony, though. It'd be between Helen, that-thing-which-may-or-may-not-be-God, and me.

It was going to happen at 6:30 this evening. I even called my parents to tell them of my plans, though I had no intention of offering invites. I just let them know that my life of sin would soon be over because Helen and I were to be married, and, after that, they could enter my house without fear of heavenly reprisals or feelings of remorse for their lost and wayward son. They didn't say anything substantial. Mom just sobbed on the phone while dad farted in the background.

I put down the receiver and realized, at that moment, that I didn't need their approval. I'd never been lost and wayward; Helen and I had never lived in sin. If anyone, it was my mother and father living in sin, in a passionless and sexless union.

Still, I was unable to use the hole until things were official. I told myself that it was the fear of my own body and not feelings of guilt that held me back, realizing that to harbor guilt would be to admit that my love for Helen was wrong, which would only vindi-

13

cate my parent's opinion of our relationship. I refuse to give them that satisfaction. I refuse to let them steal my joy.

But what if they were always right, and I always wrong? I've been thinking—being trapped in bedroom ruins, at the very least, gives one time to think—and now wonder if I deserve this. Maybe our love *is* Satan-born and that-thing-which-may-or-may-not-be-God is cursing my house and me, cursing us with death.

No, that's crazy. I've got to get hold of myself. But I can't. It's too easy to regress and feel guilty, empty, scared, horrible, and dead. My body is a momentary chamber that's too easily vacated. It's hollow—like a reed or a lute, and feels sucked clean, all sticks and bones bound by dry meat.

Maybe it's karma. Admitting this is painful, but I scarred Helen once; *really* scarred her, I mean, physically and emotionally. No relationship is perfect, but what I did was *unthinkable*.

That day, I sensed Helen was in a pissy mood. I swept her floors eight different times, beginning at eight different startpoints and traveling along eight different vertices on eight different angles, yet none of these things seemed to please her. Eventually, I could take no more. I ran to the kitchen, brandished a knife taken from the sink, and stabbed her walls, stabbed them twice.

That happened exactly two years, three months, twenty-seven days, four hours, twenty-three minutes, and six seconds ago. Perhaps I'd done worst things, but THE STABBING OF HELEN—(I think of it in all uppercase letters)—is the one event that sticks in my mind and makes me feel rotten to the core, like a foaming animal or dried out stump. I wish I could fashion a whip studded with fragments of soft drink cans. I'd lash myself with it. I imagine myself doing just that—desirous of hundreds if not thousands of cuts—but the first imagined lash hurts like a mother. It takes all I've got to imagine a second.

Imagining a third is impossible.

God, I'm so tired, more tired than I've ever known. This is a tiredness that seeps into bones and makes them sag. My marrow feels corrupted.

Before I shut my eyes, I reach out to Helen one last time. It's mostly mental, as only three fingers of my left hand can move. I touch exposed timbers with them, and focus, focus hard. The world becomes a fractal paradise behind my eyelids, and I enter that sublime state (*place?*) in which I'm perceptive enough to feel the subtle house spirit that enlivens her. Now, I feel nothing except my own hurt, sadness, and horror. I want to collapse in on myself and forget that I'd ever survived Helen dying on top of me.

But then I feel a pulse, just the thinnest, trickling pulse of Helen, alive in there and with me. If I die tonight, she'll see me through the many darkened corridors my soul will encounter. In this understanding, I find peace enough to dream.

CHAPTER TWO

State and Fifth.

These words are in my head when I awake. Don't know why I'm thinking them. They don't seem connected to a dream—or anything else for that matter—nor do they sound like my voice. Before, the thoughts in my head had always sounded like me.

Sunlight's back, too much of it. I shut my eyes and don't see the warm and gunky something that drips into my mouth, tasting of liquefied road-kill. My hand moves up (*moves up?*) to my face. A thick and oily sheen covers everything but my forehead.

I open my eyes, look around. The ceiling no longer hovers above me; the roof now does that job. What little remains of the ceiling is rippled and riddled with defects, not unlike the hide of a brittle carcass. Little round mushrooms of decay have erupted on it, exuding moisture that drips from pulsing, spiral clusters resembling sea anemones.

I remain in bed for some time after I awake, even as clusters weep. Had Helen gotten sick and died, and, if possible, could a house illness mutate into people illness, spread, and create pandemic conditions?

No matter. Thoughts of worldwide superdeath don't concern me. With Helen dead, I'd almost welcome it.

I sit up. Sagging ceiling remains tear against my body, unleashing dust. Helen's materials have converted to a husk consistency—like shredded wheat—and dry-rotted overnight. The smell isn't husk-like, though. It reminds me more of rancid bacon fat than the processed wheat cereals of my youth.

When I leave the bed, my feet touch down not on the floor, but in the crawlspace. Boards have all cracked, broken through, and rotted away.

I cringe. So many gooey things on the crawlspace floor: some shaking and shambling, others dead and in various states of decay. One—ensconced in a corner near the closet—looks like the skeleton of a small, misshapen human, but not a child.

There is plant life, too—squishy, fungoid, and abundant. I hadn't known such plants existed. I try not to step on them, as they feel like Wet Death beneath my toes.

I trudge on, tearing through dry-rotted boards and beams and assorted crawlspace horrors, bringing forth more of that horrible smell, until I reach the dresser. The disease that had decimated Helen's structure hadn't infected her furnishings.

There, I run my index finger up and down my crotch and bring it to my nose. My boxers are no longer damp, but my finger smells of ammonia. Thankfully, my ass is no longer sticky. I'd felt sweat earlier, not shit.

I take off my underwear and remove a fresh pair from the dresser, boxers printed with cartoon lobsters and palm fronds. Inappropriate perhaps, but it's the only pair that isn't dirty or riddled with strange holes. A few appear as though teams of moths have eaten at them. I wonder if the same disease that killed my house is now killing my underwear.

I put the boxers on and walk to the closet. Going about the same dresser-to-closet routine I'd do on any other morning feels weird but comforting. I may never again have a morning routine, so I should enjoy it while it lasts.

Dressed, I stand at the edge of my bedroom wall with eyes closed. I don't want to plow through the rotten remains of my house—it would be like stabbing Helen again, this time with my body—but all her windows and doors are folded in on themselves or collapsed into tiny, pinpoint apertures.

I hold my nose and push against the wall. Ex-wood is thicker than the ceiling and takes a while to crinkle and snap. I pass paneling, then sheetrock. I'm inside Helen now, but not in a desirable way. Her outside was dry, but her interior feels wet like a chest cavity or womb.

I tear through the death-wet wood of the house and past molten vinyl siding into a glaring and emerald day. The sky hadn't looked so green viewed through my shattered ceiling. Perhaps the wall is a womb and it has birthed me into a new reality. Grass is deep red and, in places, black, but this isn't a dead black. It's vibrant and alive. Trees grow where they've been rooted for years, but they've lost all substance, becoming shadow-things. I wonder if my hands would go through them if I were to touch their anti-bark, then a slightly less rational thought intrudes: *would they get angry if I tried?*

Beyond the backyard, things seem increasingly different, though how different I cannot say. I rarely leave Helen through her back door—I feel almost naughty thinking 'back door'—so the backyard and the landscape beyond are still strange worlds to me. A hill arises about a hundred yards beyond my house, red-black and sharp looking. It's hard to tell, especially from a distance, but a thread that runs from top to bottom appears to be a sulfurous, orange waterfall.

I look up, away from the waterfall. Orange clouds bend and stretch like bands of fluffy elastic. The sky that contains them ripples. I imagine getting caught up in these skywaves and letting their singular frequency overtake me.

18

That might prove dangerous, so I keep my attention focused no higher than the top of the average shadow tree.

When I turn back to Helen, my heart feels ruptured and bloody. She's collapsed entirely, her middle sagging into the ground like a rain-swollen tarp stretched over a cavernous sinkhole. Seeing her in this condition reminds me of my old house which, though intact, felt as dead as Helen the day I moved out. I miss it so much, especially now that Helen is gone. Though it said or did nothing, it was my best friend during childhood. I was especially fond of the little room in the attic. I want to go there again, back to the imagined ghosts and dusty moats floating listlessly in sunbeams.

I stop thinking such thoughts; they're counterproductive.

In the front yard, I see that the neighboring houses are in the same state as mine, collapsed and stinking of bacon fat. Maybe a house illness *is* going around, a particularly virulent one.

I feel sad for these homes, but only because they are (*were?*) Helen's brothers and sisters. I never knew them like I knew her, never got to experience their unique essences. Seeing them in this state is akin to seeing the corpses of human strangers at a mass funeral. In the face of emptiness, I can feel only nebulous, detached sorrow.

No cars have passed in at least fifteen minutes. My neighbors (I almost thought of them as 'neighbots' again) are probably still trapped in their respective houses. I should go over, offer assistance. It'd be the *human* thing to do.

But what if this is all part of a conspiracy cooked up in their collective head? I hadn't figured this might be a ploy to get me inside one of their homes. But why would they destroy their own property to get at me? And how was such destruction possible? They'd have to be in cahoots with someone, but whom? The Red Cobra-Head Commandos?

Regardless, my civic duty can't be ignored; I must come

to the aid of my fellow man, even if my fellow man is a soulless bot, even if the thought of leaving my property makes my hands tingle.

Crossing the street is like approaching a foreign country or, better yet, nearing the boundary of outer space. Turning, I see Helen behind me, strangely comforting even in her sagging decay. Years have passed since I left her to do more than pick up food, drinks, or toiletries. Since she came into my life, I hadn't needed to engage the outside world on a meaningful level.

I walk around Harold's yard, not casing the joint, but deciding on a point of entrance. The usual method won't suffice. The roof and ceiling above the front porch have melted over the door, and I doubt I could plow through debris so thick. Eventually, a man-sized defect in the rear of the house proves viable.

I enter a storage room. Things are all hidden away in boxes upon which a bright and fluorescent moss grows. When I look at it from one angle, the moss appears blue. From another, it appears green. Like my own, Harold's house has no floor. His crawlspace is weirder, though. Brown whirlpools swirl and make gurgling sounds, eight in this room alone. I don't notice many skeletons. Most, I assume, have sunk into the quicksand that surrounds and feeds the vortexes. I step quickly, otherwise, my feet might never leave the muck.

The door to the hallway isn't even a foot high. Streams of what appear to be hardened snot drape to the floor from the top of the bowed facing, making the now tiny entrance look like the gate to a cage. The snot bars are easily snapped. Once they're gone, I squeeze my body through the aperture, mucking up clothes and scraping skin from my back

I remain on fours across the hall and into the only room accessible from that point. The ceiling here looks like a rain heavy tarp upon which abundant life grows. I swat at fungoid things more aggressive than those growing on Helen. They pulse rhythmically and squirt black ink at me. One in particular has long, swinging flagella, but I don't get near it, as I imagine the protrusions might be dangerous, like stingers on a jellyfish.

The ceiling conceals almost everything in the room beneath a sagging canopy. I take at least ten steps inside before I notice the bed through a defect.

Harold's supine on the mattress, wearing only the socks and underwear he'd slept in. A wood beam had gored his anus— probably as his house fell—penetrated his body cavity, and exited his mouth. Poor dead Harold: my ass aches sympathetically as my stomach turns. The guy's black and green and blue and bloated, like he's been dead a month.

I notice how his corpse wears a tin foil hat. Perhaps he wasn't lying and did, in fact, have a strange skin condition that rendered sunrays deadly. But what if someone had put that particular helmet on him *after* he died? Who would do such a thing?

But I can no longer hold back vomit, and heaving quiets my suspicious mind. When finished, I don't wipe my mouth; I plow headlong into the wall. It only hurts a little, and, ultimately, it's better than contending with mucky vortexes. They grow wider the longer I stay in the dead man's house.

Against my better judgment, I try four other homes, as they're the only ones I can still breach. The occupants are corpses in three; the last dwelling is empty. I don't continue the search.

On my way home, I pass a house whose prior existence is evinced by only five front steps and a sidewalk. A whirlpool has

21

eaten the rest, one that swirls as long and as wide as the foundations that once stood there. When I go for a closer look, the air is sucked out of my mouth and nostrils. I get as far as the paper box before deciding it unwise to continue.

The day is even more emerald (*emeralder?*) upon my return, and Helen is really, *really* dead, dead and gone. So dead, she has converted into an oozing and bubbling sludge pool in my absence. Steam rises from her muck, and heat waves bake me if I stand too close.

I get down on my hands and knees, as near as I can get without dying. "Please come back," I implore. "I'll do anything. I'll clean you more often. I'll even put new carpet in you. Beautiful, expensive carpet!"

Helen just makes a noise that sounds like *glug*. I want to rake at my chest until my heart is exposed. How could she do this to me, after all I've done? Perhaps our love was always single-sided and I've been deceiving myself for years.

It's against my fundamental nature but—God help me—I begin to hate her.

Is she cheating on me? But how can she cheat when she can't move on her own volition? No matter. I *know* she's cheating.

Had Helen sent out mind rays or thought beams to perspective suitors, and did they come to put their thingies into the hole that I drilled for myself while I was away, buying yogurt, muffins, and milk at the grocery store? Was Harold one of them? Did my house find him *hotter* than me? Did he have a bigger and more satisfying penis?

"You bitch!" I scream. "You horrible, awful bitch!"

I hate myself for calling her that.

"Fuck you!"

Then I hate myself more, but can't stop.

"Fuck you! Fuck you! Fuck you! I don't love you and never will!"

A sudden smooth and husky voice behind me: "Hey, man."

I turn quickly. The stranger in the road reminds me of a black Man-at-Arms from the He-Man toys, complete with metallic chest plate and matching helmet, stretchy green pants showcasing muscular thighs, and an obscenely bulging codpiece studded with little gems that glisten in the sun.

"Catch you at a bad time?" he asks.

I turn back around, not wanting to face him. "You might say that."

I hear footsteps and turn around. He's crossing the street. I don't want him—or anyone else—on my property, but I'm too weak to resist.

"What's wrong, boy?"

"Can't you fucking see?"

The man (*at arms*?) looks down at Helen. "Yeah, but you're not alone. A lot of people lost their shit today."

I say nothing, because I know I'm alone—more alone than I've ever been—and no one has lost more than me.

"Why don't you go back to your own place? Leave me with mine."

"I don't have a *place*. The streets are my home..."

Great, a crazy homeless person—just what I need. I check my pockets for change or a small bill to pacify him, but I've left all my money in Helen.

"...and I want to invite you to walk them with me, all the way to State and Fifth."

The intersection sounds familiar. Then I remember it's the one I'd had in my head when I woke up. "Oh," I respond, and leave it at that. Nothing seems important or in any way meaningful without Helen.

He creeps in closer. Five more feet, and we could touch. "I have a feeling we may find something there, but we have to go to find it."

My skin feels prickly. "I just want to stay here with my house, thank you very much."

"It'll be good for you, and I could use the company."

My temples begin to pulse. "Nothing will do me good, and I don't care what you can use! Leave me alone!"

The man looks disappointed. "Son, you gotta get control of your inner heart-piece so you can mount the happy champion."

"*What?*"

"Those are the words in my head now, and I've found the words in my head are always the right ones to say."

My hands clench. Bile churns in my liver. I feel what must be a hate gland forming near my left tonsil, one that wells up with toxic and vile fluids I'll surely spit at this man if he dares touch me. "And how might I mount this *happy fucking champion?*"

"By slapping on your spurs and riding in the saddle, riding high."

"That doesn't make a damn bit of sense."

"It doesn't have to, man. Just go with it."

"I really don't think I'd be comfortable mounting the happy champion. Thanks anyway; fuck off." I turn back to Helen and imagine silver filaments that extend from my hands in runners and penetrate her molten pit. Perhaps my visualization will be strong enough to enliven her, but I doubt it. I'm just desperate, and my concentration is broken soon enough by the unwanted stranger:

"But the happy champion would feel comfortable mounting you if you let him into your heart, though it might hurt—might even be *painful*—to grant him space therein."

I want this guy not only off my property, but off the very face of the Earth. He's taking me away from Helen when she needs me most (*when I need her most?*). He's a bad influence, a bad man. I'd pluck his eyes out with my tongue and eat them if I could. "No, I will not leave! *Never!* I will die and rot here"—my eyes bulge—"with Helen, *forever!*"

"Never let it be said that I force anyone's hand." The man turns away. "I won't bother you anymore."

"Okay, bye-bye then," I say, my words steeped in venom. The man starts down the street, but I don't watch him leave. I turn back to Helen instead.

Though I abandoned her for only a few seconds, she's become an even more horrible thing, a vile and disgusting corpse, radiating horror. Dense patches of mold cover her molten bulk, the consistency of which has taken on the form (and smell) of spoiled milk or cottage cheese. The *glug* now sounds thin and reedy, but it also sounds like speech. *Leave me,* it seems to say.

"No," I get down on my hands and knees, wishing I could adopt Helen's pain. "I can't and I won't!"

The gas escapes again, making that same maddening sound.

"Never! Never! Never!"

I'm shouting so loudly that I almost miss the next noise she makes. It's as thin and reedy as the first, but says something different: *Find why.*

Suddenly, I understand...

The only reason I'd survived was to somehow make sense of this tragedy. And yes, I'll find why; this I promise to Helen. I will not rest until I know the answers.

I say my final goodbyes, make my final promises, and walk out into the street. I look for the man, but he's nowhere to be seen. It's not that I want to be with him, or with anybody for that matter. I just don't want to travel through this strange new world alone. I curse my inherent distrust of automobiles.

"Crazy man," I shout. "Crazy man!"

"Right behind you."

I jump. "Where the hell did you come from?"

"Nowhere in particular." He starts walking.

I follow close behind. Though I don't want to engage him in any way, my eyes keep wandering to the side of the road, to weird red shadows that duck and dart between groves of shadow trees lining the road, and to bushes that seem to have faces if I look too long at them. Perhaps conversation will distract me from such things.

I struggle to come up with something—*anything*—to say. It's been so long since I've addressed another human on a semi-meaningful level; I'm not sure I can manage it. "I never got your name," I say. "Mine's Carlos."

"Mine's Tony. I'm a *Protector of the Neighborhood*, one of many."

"Is that a job title?"

"Yes, it's my duty to keep peace, maintain beauty, and groove with the splendor that radiates from all things bright and beautiful. The Mission Command-Control Commander (or the MC-CC) gave me this motto upon my creation; it's been mine ever since."

"So, what do you—uh—defend against?"

"Quasi-dimensional psychopomps and multi-arrayed spectra." A self-assured look spreads across his face. "And I kill them with my guns."

Firearms scare me. "You have guns?"

"I have these." He flexes insanely large biceps. "And this." He grabs his insanely large package. "They're the only guns I need."

I am only partially relieved. "Okay, well, that's great and all, but perhaps you should try protecting elsewhere. The alien menace isn't too strong here."

"You don't know shit, boy. The alien menace here is stronger than you can imagine. If not for me, your neighbors would have been dead years sooner." He pauses, looks at me. "And you'd be dead, too."

"I really don't think—"

"Have you ever been murdered in your home?"

"I'm alive now, aren't I?"

"How about your wife? Has she ever been raped by invisible assailants?"

"I don't have a human wife."

"That's not the point. Have things of extraterrestrial origin ever interrupted you while masturbating?"

"Do you mean while I was masturbating, or while they were?"

"Either or."

"Can't say they have."

His eyes twinkle. I didn't realize eyes could do that outside of movies. "Then I've done my job."

"If you do all this stuff, then why've I never seen you?"

"Because I fight in an overlapping dimension." He looks around, taking in the green sky, red grass, and shadow trees. "But, since yesterday, I've not been able to tell the two dimensions apart."

"So, you protect people from darkness and evil?"

"It's Mission Objective Number One, or MONO."

"But you do nothing to protect their houses."

"Protecting houses is outside the job description. I'm a Defender, not an insurer."

The man's presence is starting to sicken me. "You can be

glib about it because you never had a home to lose!"

"My profession requires that I be homeless."

"Your profession is useless if it can't save Helen!"

He stops walking. "There was nothing I could do about it, okay. I fight psychopomps and multi-arrayed spectra, and neither of these had anything to do with this house shit. If they had, I would have poked it in the rear."

"Don't you mean 'nip it in the bud'?"

He doesn't reply, just stares off into the distance.

"You don't have to be rude."

"*Sssssh!* I'm not being rude; I'm detecting something."

I follow his gaze to a scarecrow in a field. There are no fields in this part of the city, just small personal lots bordered by woods.

"Tony, is it safe?"

He says nothing, just continues to watch the scarecrow thing.

"Tony—"

"*Hush!* It's moving now."

I don't see it move. In fact, I no longer see it at all. "It's okay, Tony. It's not even there anymore."

"It's not there"—his eyes and neck veins bulge—"because it's here!"

The air around us shimmers in a patch nearly eight feet tall and five feet wide. Then, the thing appears, pulsing with malevolence. It glares down at me with rotten corpse eyes, looking like nothing I've ever seen, not even in movies: a leather and chain clad zombie-monster-serpent-ape-predator-thing enhanced with bionic parts and fused with twisted strips of metal and coiled strands of thick, pulsing wire. I can't turn away; I have to stare as the thing exhales red steam from six asymmetrical nostrils.

Rather than being terrified, Tony seems annoyed in the

face of such stark and unending horror. "I thought I dealt with you yesterday." He smirks arrogantly. "But you're back for more *sexpounding.*"

The thing recoils, as if the word had triggered a particularly bad childhood memory. It breaks its connection with me, and I take cover behind a scraggly bush laden with red berries that throb like small, synchronized drums.

I look on from relative safety as Tony charges the thing. Running, his body loses form, becoming fluid and silver like mercury. When it reaches the monster, it coils around the thing's neck and lower legs. When Tony reappears—his physical body in the same position as his fluid body—he has the monster in a headlock. With that arm, he gives its neck a *tightsqueeze.* I don't know how I know this maneuver is called a *tightsqueeze.* I just do.

Once the creature is limp but not fully unconscious, he flips open his bejeweled codpiece. With one hand, he pulls down the horrible thing's pants. He uncoils himself with the other. "Are you ready for this, baby?"

The thing isn't at all ready, but Tony doesn't care. His eyes roll back as he thrusts himself into a gnarled and warty ass. He pumps his hips with a fluid, circular motion as his hands rub up and down the creature's body. No longer malevolent, its eyes are now bugging, pleading. It cries out to no avail.

"Take it, you bitch!" Tony hisses, spit flying from his lips. "Take every smooth black inch of it! Yeah!"

The thing takes every smooth black inch of it.

"Take it for peace, then take for beauty," he continues. "Groove with its splendor!"

The thing shakes as though stricken with epilepsy. A lumpy piss-colored foam pours from its maw. The front of its leathery trousers tent out, but it's not aroused. Tony's member is just exiting out the other side. In time, it starts heaving and hitching, smoke curling from its ears.

A *sexpounding*, I now know, is horrible beyond belief.

Tony concludes with a series of violent jabs, after which he unleashes a loud and protracted groan. Finally, he withdraws, and the thing falls to the street where it decomposes to dust.

I watch Tony wipe sweat from the dense and twisting *afrocurls* protruding from his helmet. He coils himself back up, closes his codpiece, and walks over to the bush where I hide.

"I'm delicious even when fighting," he says, pushing twigs back to reveal my pallid, quaking form. "Sure as shit, baby. Sure as shit."

"So, uh, can I come out now?"

"Oh yeah. Never takes long to dispose of your neighborhood's garbage." He outstretches a warm and calloused hand, and I accept it. I rise to my feet, but my legs are unsteady and my head swims.

"Do you mind if I wait a few seconds before we go on? I —I just—just—"

"I understand, man. Take all the time you need. It's not as though we have an appointment to keep."

A few minutes pass, and my bearings return—at least as much as they'll *ever* return—and we continue on. I turn to Tony. "You won't ever—uh—*sexpound* me, will you?"

He smiles; his teeth are very clean. "Of course not."

"Thanks. I just needed to hear that."

"*Sexpounding* isn't for okay guys like you."

His words humble me. "I'm sorry for thinking you were insane, Tony. I guess I owe my life to you."

"Think nothing of it. I just do my job, and do it well."

CHAPTER THREE

We continue our walk, the day even brighter than it'd been when we started. And the street, it seems to ramble on for entirely too long. Maybe it just seems that way because all the houses are gone, but we really should have reached the turn off ages ago.

In time, I begin to wonder if perhaps this is the only street that still exists, that all other streets have morphed into this one, and that, if I were to backtrack, I would no longer be able to find my way to Helen. Every mile would look the same until I died on my feet.

Panic wells. Then I notice something on the road, followed by a distant rumbling sound. It's just a dot in the distance, and now I'm certain my street has lengthened.

I worry that it might be another quasi-dimensional psychopomp, but Tony's behavior doesn't indicate anything's amiss. Soon, I realize it's some sort of automobile—maybe a large van.

The vehicle reaches us and grinds to a halt. It looks like a bus that might have ran a downtown route thirty or forty years ago. It rattles, clanks, sputters, and I wonder how it made it this far out without breaking down. Then I wonder why it's here in the first place; my street has no bus route.

The door swings open. A driver sits at the wheel. Thin,

middle-aged, non-assuming, he wears a blue button-up shirt and black pants. For a second, his eyes appear to be windows, complete with panes and facing. When he speaks—shouting to be heard over the din of the motor—the illusion shatters. His thick southern accent sounds affected, and I wonder if this man has something to hide.

"Where you boys goin'?"

"State and Fifth, man," Tony says.

"Fancy that. State and Fifth is the only stop on my route."

"But you're going the wrong way," I say.

"I know. We'll turn around once you get on, but I had to pick you guys up first. Today is a special day, and this is a special route."

I'm apprehensive, but Tony boards without hesitation. I follow him up the steps. The last thing I want is to get left behind.

Inside, it looks like a very old and unloved school bus. The walls are metal, painted green, and big two-person seats are covered in brown, cracked vinyl. It's filled to capacity, but the other passengers are all cardboard cutouts overlaid with life-size photographs trimmed to fit their backings.

"Has your bus always been this weird," I ask the driver.

His voice is jolly. "Nope, it just got its weird on yesterday!"

"Oh, okay. Do we owe you anything?"

"Just give me your tickets."

"But we don't have—"

Smiling, the driver snatches a ticket from Tony's hand, then from my own, and drops both into his coat pocket.

"Wait! How did you—"

"Thanks, that's all I need. Go find a seat now." He points to the back of the bus, and his arm, for a second, looks like a 2x4. "I can't pull out until you do. Safety regulations."

"But they're all filled." I recognize that the passengers are cardboard and could be easily moved, but something—I don't know what—makes me think that moving them might be a bad idea, that they might get *upset* if their seats were stolen.

The driver's tone is matter-of-fact: "I think you overlooked a couple spots."

I turn again and see there's indeed an empty two-person seat in the rear of the bus. I nod at the driver and follow Tony to the back where we take our seat in front of a cardboard man and woman. Are they strangers, I wonder, or husband and wife? Maybe they're lovers...

No matter. I look towards the driver. At least he's real. Or rather I think he is. From the back, he almost looks like a cutout, too.

Tony doesn't seem weirded out by this. Wish I could be more like him. Ultimately, looking at my hands is the most comforting thing I can do.

"I'm glad I could share this ride with you," Tony says as the bus starts up and turns around. "Now we can relax and get to know each other better."

"No offense, but I'd rather just relax right now. Been through a lot today."

Tony continues as though he hadn't heard me. "When I first laid eyes on you, I knew I was seeing *A Brother From Another Mother*, ABFAM for short. That's what we call people who, despite being genetically human, share characteristics, and even essences, of the Defenders."

I look up from my hands. "I'm one of those people?"

"Of course. Our pet name for your kind is *Abfammy*, so from this point on I will call you *Abfammy Carlos* due to my friendship and love for you."

"Can you just call me Carlos while thinking of me as

Abfammy Carlos?"

"I guess that would work."

As Tony continues to wax friendly, I settle in and try to relax and let the vibrations of the bus give me a mild boner, but I keep thinking of Helen and how she must now look. A better homeowner would have done *something* to avert her abysmal fate.

I barely hear Tony over the roar and tumult of my brain. A relaxing bus ride isn't going to happen. Even the cardboard cut-outs sense my internal chaos. I see faces now, not just the backs of heads.

Tony senses my unease, too. "You don't have to speak. I sense exactly what's wrong." He shakes his head. "You can't let another control you, even when that thing is a house. Claim your birthright and be a man. Bitches come and bitches go."

"Excuse me?"

"Bitches come and bitches go. It boils down to that."

Red and black spots fill the bus; my brain is electric with rage: "I don't care if you've saved my life everyday in my old neighborhood, nobody—*nobody*—calls Helen a bitch!" Then I flail in my seat, for doing so is preferable to hitting such a large and imposing man.

Tony is unfazed. "I'm going to go ahead and lay it on straight for you, okay. Are you ready for it?"

Continued flailing is my only response.

"Your house is dead, man. Sorry to have to tell you, but it's true. It's a real goner."

"Her!" I rage. "She's a *her* not an it!"

"She's a real goner, okay. But semantics don't change *facts*. You can cry and you can mourn, but nothing's going to bring it—her—back. She's just a memory now, and no one can live in a memory."

"But can't you see? Memories are the only things that matter anymore!"

"You know what you really need right now?"

"Helen back, or at least a damn good explanation."

"Nah, man." His eyes bore into me. "What you really need is a backrub."

"Excuse me?"

"It'll do you good." He reaches his hands out. Fingers crinkle and make popping sounds. "Trust me."

"I said I don't want one!"

He smiles, his teeth somehow brighter than before. "But you're going to get one, baby."

"Rape," I shout. "Rape!" But no one listens, for they are cardboard.

Hands clamp down on my shoulders. I push myself forward, but can't break his grip. When he kneads, I imagine his hands slowly making their way up my neck, where they will surely knead harder. But something changes, and his ministrations begin to feel good. All my cares and worries flow downstream. Then utter weirdness kicks in, and I begin to ... but there are no words to describe what I'm feeling now.

"How about 'groove with the sensation,'" Tony offers, seemingly reading my mind.

It sounds strangely apropos. I nod my head, suddenly a difficult act, it feels as though it's floating miles above my neck.

"Now talk. Tell me everything. Release pain."

"I – I—"

"Only reveal what you feel comfortable telling me. I won't pressure you." He rubs my back harder, really getting to the heart of my tension. A mental block lifts, fractal patterns explode behind my closed lids, and I hear monks—Benedictine, Cistercian, or Satanic, I cannot say—chanting in the distance.

"So," he continues, "what is it about your house—Helen
—that makes her different from the others? Why is she special,
apart from the fact you lived in her?"

"She's the love of my life."

"And did she love you back?"

"I—I think. After today, I'm not so sure." Tony's knead-
ing hands find their way into my soul, and words flow freely. "She
had every reason to love me, though. I did *everything* for her! I
had I LOVE MY HOUSE banners printed and put on Helen's
outside. Once, I even tried to get a chapter of the *Man House
Love Association* going. No one was interested."

"Really?"

"Really. And I'd walk up to people on the street and ask,
'Have you loved your house today?' Sometimes they'd ignore
me; other times they'd punch me. But there was one man that I
thought understood. He didn't turn away when I gave him the
leaflets. He took them, never trashing them like the others."

"Did you take him under your wing?"

"I had every intention, but then I realized he was only
interested in getting me to sign a contract for a video he was pro-
ducing, something about bums fighting. He wanted me to be the
referee."

"That's cold, man. I might've smashed him into the ground
for that."

"I was insulted, don't get me wrong. I'm not the kind of
person he thought I was. I'm no kook."

"Of course you're not."

I open my eyes, and, for a second, Tony's face isn't a
face at all, but a beautiful swirling vortex into which all my pain
and suffering disappears. Seconds later, he's a man again, but his
face wavers and hitches. "Really," I say. "You believe that?"

"Yes, and I believe I understand now. You feel alone because no one understands you, and this is true, but that makes you special. Also, you're in deep mourning. You've lost someone you love; you're tender now—so very tender. I should respect that, but I should help you find the courage to step out of your misery, too."

"Just help me find out what happened to Helen."

"I'll do my best," Tony lifts his hand from my shoulders. It's like going from full-blown trip to baseline in an instant, and I spend a few minutes sagging into the seat, breathing deeply. I'm not over Helen—don't imagine I'll ever be—but feel cleaner having unloaded on Tony.

"I'm sorry for giving you so much heck," I say, and realize this is the second time I've apologized in less than an hour. "Didn't mean anything by it, really."

He smiles. "And I know you didn't, but this is my favorite part of the job—bringing a little light into one man's life. That life was yours today, baby."

Nobody had ever called me baby. I feel touched, warm on the inside, and freaked out, all at the same time.

"In fact, I want to share something with you, since you shared something with me. Do I have your permission?"

I nod.

"My name pronounced *Tony* but spelled *R'yony*. You are the only non-Defender who knows this."

"I'm honored you'd tell me."

The bus makes another stop. This time, the driver—who no longer looks like a cutout—exits the bus. When he returns, he carries a cardboard person. He places it in an empty seat—which I *know* wasn't there previously—and walks away with the thing's ticket in his pocket.

I wonder if these cardboard people see themselves as real and all others—Tony and I included—as cardboard, but that's not something I want to think about.

So I don't.

Instead, I look out the window, glad to have gotten the window seat. We pass another person trying to build a replacement house out of what appears to be Twinkies, another from tiny twigs, or perhaps matchsticks. I'm glad the bus doesn't stop for them. What they're doing is a mockery, and I hate it (and them).

A few miles later, we go up a hill, though there's no hill between my place and downtown. We travel up it just the same and drive through woods for a while. The road here is so narrow that branches of shadow trees first tickle, then breach the bus' hull. I duck down and put my head between my legs, imagining I might otherwise be decapitated. Then I notice that, like true shadows, these branches have no substance. No longer afraid of losing my head, I look out over the woods and see a reddish brook by which a fawn drinks. Something doesn't look quite right with the fawn—it's oddly misshapen, lumpy. A little further up the road, all I see are shadow trees. They're so tall here; I can't see their tops. One defecates copiously through an opening between long and gangly roots.

"Sure wish I had my camera," R'yony says to himself.

But I turn away. A shitting tree is something I don't want to see again.

Outside of the woods, and on the other side of the heretofore non-existent hill, the bus makes a stop. The driver helps yet another cardboard cutout onboard. Now, I wonder if he had to help R'yony and me onboard too, and that we only imagined ourselves walking to our seats, but I don't want to think about this, either.

I stare out the window. Seems our bus ride is coming to an end. We're very close to downtown now, or, rather, the remains of it.

Streets remain drivable, but pavement has given way to brick and cut stone, like how it might have looked before the motorcar came. Above the road, the tops of bigger businesses are intact, but their bases have deflated into puddles of brick or steel mush. Buildings nearest a large, centrally located mansion aren't decaying as quickly as their brethren and feature only a healthy sprinkling of cavities. Perhaps close proximity to the mansion bathes their corpses in ethereal embalming fluid. The mansion itself squats atop a number of major city streets and businesses. A lot of people have gathered in its proximity and slightly beyond, perhaps too many of them.

The driver turns around. "Sorry, but it's very crowded, and I can't take you all the way to State and Fifth. You'll have to walk the rest of the way to the mansion, but it'll only be about five blocks." When he turns back, he looks like a cutout again.

We pass through the crowd for a few minutes, taking out a handful of onlookers along the way. Outside my window, there's nothing but a sea of bopping heads and flailing arms. It looks like a street party, only not quite so fun. When the bus finally stops, I don't want to get out. I hate crowds, and this one will surely swallow me whole.

The door opens. Cardboard cutouts disappear one by one until R'yony and I are the only passengers on the bus. Suddenly, we're outside it, too. When I turn around, I no longer see the bus. Don't even hear it.

And a wall of stark raving humanity surrounds us. One of the people beside me looks like a cardboard man from the bus, and that's yet another thing I don't want to think about. I turn from him, but no matter where I look, I encounter faces.

Surely, at least one of these belongs to someone who knows what happened, but those who don't look possessed look psychotic and those who don't look psychotic look depressed. I don't want to speak to anyone here, which, of course, sends an electromagnetic signal out to all the wrong people.

For the most part, those who accost me don't sound like they're speaking English, or any other language with which I have a passing familiarity. One man in particular hisses and foams, but at least I can make out what he's saying:

"Oh howling monkey shit! Howling, flying flailing monkey shit! Glistening, effervescent amber waves of monkey shit! Monkey shit sundae surprise ala mode!" He grabs a hold of my shirt and leans into my face, breath noxious. I look for R'yony, but he's nowhere to be seen. "How many other ways can I express it," the man continues. "What will make you understand? What if I said *I'm fucking fuck fucked*? Would that work? Would it!"

My voice quakes. "It might."

"Yeah, that's what I—" His eyes narrow to angry slits. "Wait, are you the one?"

"Am I the one what?"

"The one who took my fucking house!"

"No, mine was taken, too!"

He wraps thick and meaty hands around my shoulders, his grip sweaty yet strong. "You've got it in your head, don't yah? Yeah, that's right. My house in your fucking head!" His hands slide up from my shoulders to my neck, but they're not gentle like R'yony's.

"Please, don't—"

He wrings my neck. I can't breathe; my head pounds, and everything looks blue save the red foam forming around the man's mouth.

His voice is high-pitched and shrill, like a machine gone insane: "Give it back! Give it back! Give it back you motherfuckingfuckerfuck!" Smoke curls out of his ears as blood shoots from his eyes, ears, and nose. With a loud pop, his head explodes.

When he falls, R'yony kicks his body aside. The crowd swallows it whole.

"Did you shoot that man?"

"No, I used sub-neutrino based electro-heat vision. Works every time."

"Oh, okay."

And we continue slogging through the mess, holding hands so we might never get separated again.

Time passes, and R'yony and I are still mired in the muck. It's not quite so chaotic in the center, but I can't go more than a few feet without crashing into horrible, flailing bodies. My resolve falters.

"I don't think we can make it the rest of the way!"

"We can and we will."

"But I can't breathe, R'yony!"

I feel like giving up, letting myself fall to the pavement where my body will be stomped into bits and pieces, but then I think of Helen, and remember the mission I had obliged myself to undertake in her name.

I force myself through the maze of flesh, beating away arms and legs and torsos and parts more private, all up in my face and pulsing.

When it becomes too much, I shout as loud as I can: "I will not let you bastards bring me down! Fuck you all!" I turn around and see R'yony behind me, giving me the thumbs-up.

And this gives me the strength I need to carry on.

Two blocks later, I spot an oasis.

A group of maybe 100 people are cloistered around a

small, makeshift stage. I wonder if an invisible wall has been erected between it and the surrounding madhouse, as there's a buffer of empty space at least ten feet wide between the last row of stage-people and the beginning of chaos. For some reason, the others around me don't seem to notice this little pocket of calm.

I begin pointing and gesticulating. "I think we need to go over there."

"Seems a little sketchy. We really should get to the mansion."

"Well, I don't know about you, but I have to breathe!"

R'yony nods, but, at the same time, appears as though he's detecting something. For the moment, however, I don't care what he's detecting. I just need to break free.

At its very edge, the people-wall is force field strong. I pound my body against it, oblivious to pain, until the wall snaps and I spill out into the buffer zone.

The air smells cleaner here—no more body odor mixed with a coppery smell I fear might be blood, and I breathe it in eagerly. Even the clamoring noises behind me sound muted, like someone has dropped a damp cloth over the madhouse, smothering it.

I'm close enough to be heard by outliers in the group, though I don't know how to get their attention. I try flailing my arms and screaming. The people remain transfixed, staring at something on stage I cannot yet see.

"I don't know if I'd get much closer," R'yony says. "Things don't feel right."

But nothing will happen if I stand gawking. I ignore R'yony's advice and approach the group, though I have no idea what to say or do when I reach it. As I near the first row of listeners, I hear bits and pieces of someone's speech, or maybe it's a sermon:

"I come to you because I know I must. I'll explode otherwise, into a thousand shining pieces that twinkle and glisten." I listen for a while. Perhaps this individual knows why all the buildings have died and can help me.

"...feel static well up in your heart *sharkarakita*; feel it branch into various bodily passageways, through arteries and veins..." I groan. The speaker is a nutjob. Still, ducking into his group for a few seconds couldn't hurt. The people seem too comatose to harm me, and the street preacher (or whatever he is) might appreciate another listener in his (admittedly weird) audience. Maybe I'll even glean something from his madness.

"I'm going to move in closer," I yell to R'yony. "You can stay back if you like. I promise I won't be long."

"I'll wait," he shouts back, and then, in an entirely different tone of voice, says, "But be careful, and don't go anywhere I can't see you."

I bump against transfixed people in an attempt to incorporate myself.

"Oh, sorry," I apologize to one of them, but the person sways slightly, saying nothing. I look down. A large brown stain mars the seat of his pants. I grimace and don't stand next to him, or next to anyone whose pants feature questionable stains. There are, however, a lot of people with questionable stains, so my options are limited.

I settle on a spot and face the speaker, but not before turning the other way to make sure R'yony is still behind me. He is, but doesn't look at all pleased.

The speaker stands atop the stage, his dark hair slicked back with what looks to be motor oil. His skin is tan, wrinkly and, most of all, *greasy*. Beneath his leisure suit, his shirt is unbuttoned all the way to the base of his sternum. Vile chest hair emanates from the gap like rusty steel wool.

"Don't worry," the disco-looking man continues. "You're not going to die because you're already dead. At the moment, you just aren't perceiving the dead-state, though on occasions you catch glimpses of it."

In a flash, I remember being in a zone I considered *deathspace* after drinking three large bottles of cough syrup. There, I imagined I'd been dead for so long that my bones were dust. Depressing, but then I realized how all things that had lived or would live were dead in deathspace.

The salesman's voice is louder now: "I've seen man's final end, and I've met the Death Merchants. I know who they are and the role they play in this life-that-isn't-life. The Merchants taught me many things. It wasn't a pupil-student relationship we enjoyed, however. It was a corpse-and-embalmer one."

Death Merchants. Yes, I remember them, too. I never saw them in deathspace, but felt them just the same, lurking behind swirling geodesic patterns, pulling invisible strings. I suddenly want to touch the hem of the disco-man's robe. But hadn't he been wearing 70s clothes earlier? And aren't I closer to his stage? Even R'yony seems further away. He notices my attention and shakes his head, disappointedly. A wild-eyed prophet now stands in place of the greasy disco guy, appearing as though he could reach inside me and read every sin I'd committed. His long hair billows, though there is no wind.

Spinning, I see only the top of R'yony's head above the crowd, and wonder if others perceive themselves as getting closer to the prophet. No matter. Other people are irrelevant, just shapeless blobs in the corners of my eyes.

"Carlos," the prophet says.

I stand in the front row.

"Carlos," he repeats.

Though the prophet could be addressing any Carlos, he looks directly at me. A smile forms as he notices my attention, but it's neither happy nor welcoming. It's incisive, cutting, and says he knows more about me than I'll ever know about myself.

"How do you know my name?" I don't think I've spoken these words loud enough to be heard—in fact, I might've just thought them. Nevertheless, the prophet responds.

"It doesn't matter; just die."

"But—"

"*Rot and decay and fester and bloat*!" He roars, and the air in front of his mouth ripples.

"I'm not sure I—"

The prophet shushes me. "Don't maintain your innocence. It makes you sound guilty."

"But—"

"Embrace guilt. Embrace death."

Suddenly, I'm no longer in the audience but on the stage, just inches from a man who radiates supple white energy from orifices both visible and concealed. This energy creeps towards me, entering my mouth, nose, ear, and, finally, anus.

"Think not." He touches the top of my head and allows his hand to linger, his touch making my spine come alive and whip around like an angry snake. "Rather, radiate inside my very being."

I have no choice but radiate.

"Now," he continues, pointing up at the waving, emerald sky. "I want you to look up at the skywaves. See them as they really are."

My head tilts upwards. I don't think my brain is telling it to do this. I watch as memories—all of them, even memories I

45

haven't yet had the chance to make—spool out of my head in a miles-long golden arc. Clouds part so the sky can swallow this memory chain and the body that once housed it. The sky, I realize, wants to make love to me, to tongue me and call me Daddy. *Yes, Mommy Sky. Take me.*

At that moment, a cosmic blender turns on, and I can no longer tell whether a thing had happened to me or to someone else. Light is all I see.

"Suck in the light." I hear the prophet say, somewhere. "Suck it all in."

And I do, the sensation like slurping electric spaghetti. Once I've sucked in all I can manage without exploding, the prophet appears before me, his physicality superimposed over a backdrop of fractals reminiscent of undulating, rainbow-hued corndogs.

Yes, I suddenly realize, this man *knows* what he's talking about. He's a *true prophet* and *holy man*. He'll tell me what happened to Helen, and maybe even bring her back. I want to bow by his feet, but can't because I'm floating in space sans axispoint.

"You are on your way to rebirth, Carlos," he says.

"I—I am?"

"Yes, so be glad. But first you must incorporate the following items into your wardrobe, as they will aid your transition." A folded garment appears in his outstretched left hand. "Behold, your purple underwear. Wear it until the end of your days, which will be this coming Tuesday." He outstretches his right, and a second item appears. "Behold, your personal *godglasses*. Don't put them on now. You must wait until the appointed time."

"What the hell are you talking about? This doesn't concern Helen!"

"Castration is no longer required because"—the man

pauses to look at an ethereal wristwatch—"our bodies won't live long enough to feel many sexual impulses."

It's a death cult. I have no intention of dying until I find out what happened to Helen. I hate the prophet for giving me false hope and flail my arms and legs in defiance. Hanging in space, it's all I can manage.

The corndog fractals ripple like a disturbed lake into which the prophet and the absurd things he carries disappear. Space becomes a jumble of sound and color, enveloping me, rocking my body at the same frequency as the intangible stuff around it. Only my consciousness and sense of self remain intact.

When the world settles, I stand again in the buffer zone. The prophet is on stage, still chatting away and looking like a slick, used car salesman, but he ignores me now, and that's good.

I look around for R'yony, but the Defender is gone.

CHAPTER FOUR

I'll have to make it to the mansion on my own, and that's not something I relish. Likewise, I don't relish the thought of reentering the madhouse. Thankfully, that won't be necessary. There's a velvet curtain draped door, stage left.

I walk to it, careful not to brush against anyone in the prophet's audience or listen too closely to his sermon. A sign above the curtain says *Shortcut, Please Take.*

I think of killers, thieves, big bad wolves, and other things that wait at such places. Sometimes the long way is best. I look back over the madhouse and realize such isn't the case today.

The door leads out onto an otherwise empty street lined with people who stand motionless on small, featureless lots as though they were...

... houses!

So offended, I have to run a mantra over and over in my head: *I will not fight. I will not hurt. I will not kill.*

"Like my new coat," someone asks. "I did it myself. I'm a special house."

I turn. A man stands in the yard to my left, latex dripping from him in runners. He's annoyingly persistent.

"I said do you like my new coat? It was very expensive."

I shout: "Please don't make me go over there!"

"Come on. I know you love it."

I stalk up to the man. "Frankly, it's insulting to houses to say that you are one. You're a person, and—no matter how unsavory that is—you need to get used to the fact!"

"Sorry, but I'm a house."

"Then why are you flapping your lips?"

"I'm not. You just think I am because you're crazy."

"You're the crazy one!" I collect myself. "What's your name, anyway?"

"Name?"

"And do you love the person who lives in you?"

"I'm a house, you dumb ass! Wood and brick!"

This is going nowhere, but that's exactly where I'd expected it to go. This man knows *nothing* about what it means to be a house.

He furrows his brows, something houses definitely shouldn't do. "Well, come to think of it, I guess the house I am is a he, and is named Frank, because I am a he and am named Frank."

"For the last fucking time, you are not a house!"

"I live in myself, do I not? That makes me sort of a house."

"Perhaps in a twisted way."

"Then I really don't see your problem. I'm clearly a house."

I rage at him. "No, you're a filthy and degraded human!"

"Well, you're one, too!"

The world transforms into a vortex of angry color that swirls down into a pit. I travel within various shades, riding them bareback through a dark and seemingly endless night.

When the pit vomits me out, either seconds or hours later, I hold a clump of latex-covered hair in my hand. I look up at the man. He's still pretending to be a house, but has tears in his eyes

and speaks through clenched teeth. "A house feels no pain."
I throw the clump to the ground and turn away. Nothing
to gain here, and, if I stay much longer, I might just black out and
kill the man. Don't want that on my conscience. Before I go,
however, I shout to the other house-people lining the street: "You
all be nice, quiet little homes, because I'm through fucking around!"
And they say nothing as I make my way past them, though
I hear one fart.

Ha! Houses aren't supposed to fart!

Soon, the mansion appears over a hill. The twin lines of
people-pretending-to-be-houses terminate and another line—this
one single-file—forms atop a long marble sidewalk. Most people
are turned quietly towards the mansion as though awaiting something, or perhaps they're just enraptured by the sight. It's odd
how the sidewalk ends exactly where the last man stands, but
stranger things have already happened today. The mansion looms
above us all like a god, and the air around it vibrates.

At this point, I'd expect to relish the opportunity to enter
any house— but the mansion is an odd place, multi-gabled, starkly
white, and larger than even Biltmore Estates. But size alone isn't
the source of its strangeness. It has a strong, human-like presence
reminiscent of, perhaps, a strange uncle who spends too much
time tinkering around with esoteric tools and gadgets in his base-
ment. It also radiates an increasingly visible (and increasingly blue)
aura. One of the windows appears to blink.

A few people stand off to either side of the line. Like the
crowd outside the prophet's gathering, they fail to notice what's
right beside them.

One man in particular lingers by a low-lying crater in one
of the cavity-filled buildings. Through it, I see what used to be
office space. A worker in one of the rooms still sits at his desk,
coffee mug in hand, but the same slow black rot that eats at the

building eats at him as well. The man ignores the ghastly scene to his rear. Rather, he stares intently at a cell phone clutched in his hand, looking profoundly, and perhaps terminally, sad.

"Are you, uh, okay?"

He ignores me, so I adopt another line of questioning.

"Do you know what happened to all the houses?"

Again, he ignores me. In fact, he doesn't even look up from his phone. "You haven't rung all day," he shouts. "My wife was supposed to call hours ago! My boss, too!" His voice falls to a whisper. "I don't know what's wrong. I used to get such great reception."

"Maybe phone towers are down."

He finally looks up. Eyes are red and puffy. "A day is *hell* without my ringtone!"

I want to tell him how I feel about Helen, but decide against it. "I'm sorry. I won't bother you anymore."

"Can you hum it for me?"

"Hum what?"

"My ringtone."

"Your ringtone?"

"Yes, please. Can you do that for me? It's all I ask."

"I don't know it. I—"

"Please, I'm begging you. It's an easy tune to remember, a popular song. I'm sure you've heard it. Hell, I'd hum it myself, but I don't want to seem desperate."

I never listen to the radio; I know no popular songs. A part of me wishes I'd heard every top-40 jingle available. Then I might be able to make this poor man—who is clearly a real person and not an insane, flapping thing or *neighbot*—feel better. His eyes would appear dead if not for the loss reflected in them.

"I really can't help you." I reach out and pat his back. It feels weird touching another human. "Maybe somebody else can,

51

though."

"No, it's all over now." The man rocks back and forth on his heels, clutching his cell phone like a dead baby. "All over."

I stand there for another minute, but the man has stopped speaking, save for a few muffled endearments to his phone. "I'm sorry," I say quietly, then turn away. "So sorry..."

I take a place in line, and feel like I've suddenly grown a few inches taller. I look down. The sidewalk now ends at my heels, though the man in front of me hasn't moved a step closer to the mansion.

The man behind me appears pleasant and unassuming as he looks at the cavity building to his right. "Excuse me," I ask him. "But I wonder if you might know what happened to Hel— I mean my house."

He turns to face me, slowly. "I don't, but maybe if you wait like the rest of us, we'll both find out."

I don't like the tone of this man's voice. "Wait for what?"

"Didn't you get a brochure?"

"No, was I supposed to?" I note a flyer in his hands. Its cover invites me to TOUR THE FABULOUS WONDER MANSION. "Can I see yours?"

"Get your own."

"Where?"

"There's a display case in front of the mansion. It's full of them. Can't miss it."

"Just let me see it for a second. The line is so long, and I've had a rough day."

The man exhales and, begrudgingly, hands me the brochure. "Just don't mess it up. I like to keep these things."

I look down at it. Glossy and well made, the brochure

isn't dissimilar to those found at rest stops, welcoming centers, and service stations nationwide. I open it. Inside: pictures of the mansion taken from different angles, mostly standard shots, though a few are artistically rendered. The photos were snapped recently, because the sky is emerald green and wavy and, in two of them, I note cavity buildings looming in the background, though their defects seem considerably smaller in the photographs.

Two brief paragraphs of text are both centered on the middle panel:

Experience the sights and sounds of the Wonder Mansion for free. Come in and marvel at strange (and some might say inhuman) architecture. Bathe yourself in sumptuous luxury at our famous indoor spas, and don't forget to visit our gift center. You might even learn a secret or two, provided you find yourself in the right room.

Don't let this once in a lifetime opportunity pass you by. Get in line NOW; the Wonder Mansion will be gone tomorrow, and who can say what city it'll be in next.

The last line sounds provocative. I only hope another death cult isn't hiding inside the mansion, waiting to hand me a pair of purple underwear or something equally nonsensical. Still, being the only house around, it seems the logical place to get my questions answered.

I slip the brochure in my pocket; the man eyes me. I suddenly remember it isn't mine to take. "Oh, sorry. I have a habit of doing that."

He reclaims the brochure with a harrumph.

Hours seem to pass without the line getting any shorter and the day any darker. I don't want to bother the man behind me again, as he doesn't seem like the type that likes being bothered, but he's the most convenient person, and I don't want to lose my place, as others—quite a few of them, actually—now stand behind me in line. I wonder if R'yony is somewhere back there, or maybe he beat me and is up front. Hopefully nothing bad has happened to him, but he's a big boy with *sexpounding* action and sub-neutrino based electro-heat vision, so I imagine he's taking care of himself.

"Uh, why isn't anyone going in," I ask the man in front of me.

"Because the doors won't open for a few more minutes. Didn't you read the back?"

"The back of what?"

With a sigh, the man thrusts his brochure into my hands. "Go on, look at it."

I turn the brochure over. In small print at the bottom I read: *Doors open today and today only at 9:30 PM. First come first serve.*

"Oh, now I see."

He snatches the brochure back. "I bet you do."

I draw in a deep breath—it keeps me from hitting the man—and wait. Surely whoever runs the mansion won't let everyone in at the same time; there has to be a thousand or more waiting. I may stand on the sidewalk for hours, if not days, but at least I don't have to be anywhere important.

Suddenly, I hear a whooshing sound reminiscent of a spinning helicopter propeller. The sidewalk surges forward, the man in front of me falling onto my lap, his hipbone crushing my package. I fall into the lap of the person to my rear. He groans. His package, I assume, has been crushed too. I'm glad, but only because he's a prick.

Closer, I see the mansion has a revolving glass door. It produces the helicopter sound as it whirls. People in the front of the line disappear into the blur created by the door's revolutions. Those in the middle follow quickly. The words 'salad shooter' come to mind, and I close my eyes. Want to cover my ears, too—the whooshing sounds are deafening—but my arms are pinned.

Wind produced by the door's revolutions buffets me so hard that, for a while, I think it's still blowing even after it stops. I open my eyes. Instead of the interior of a mansion, I look out over my old neighborhood, though not from an ordinary perspective. It's like seeing things from a hot air balloon, only I don't have the balloon, just the altitude.

And Helen's back, and she's alive.

I reach out, but try as I might, I can't get any closer to her. She's a mirage, and I'm a heat-stricken traveler who'll never get water.

I hear the *whoosh whoosh* of the door and turn around. One of its panels slams into me, treating my body like a pile of debris as it pushes me out of the vision of my old neighborhood and into a dark world of tessellating geometric structures. I fight against huge cubes, planes, and ridges that shoot towards me from infinity and seem like parts of one big machine. They want to crush and smother me, to seal me up in negative space, so I tear at them, rip them as though they were cardboard as I squeeze my body through impossibly narrow apertures. But there are thousands, if not millions, of layers. I keep tearing and squeezing until I forget why I'm doing these things. Finally, I see light past one of the torn boxes, come back to myself, and remember.

I fight harder against malicious geometry, hoping that I might return to my old neighborhood and way of life on the other side. Instead, I find myself in a latex and Styrofoam fantasyland, or better yet, a psychedelic children's show nightmare. There are no spas or gift shops, but the grass is composed of bright green plastic; the flowers are larger than my head, and the sky is just a blue cardboard set painted by a child.

I don't have time to orient myself (if such a thing were possible) before the ground vomits out creatures reminiscent of *Lidsville*, a Sid and Marty Krofft show whose reruns terrified me as a child. These, however, aren't hideous anthropomorphic hats, but hideous anthropomorphic houses.

One monstrosity is a painted lady house that carries a handbag roomy enough to conceal a human head. Another is a British gentleman, complete with tux and monocle. The other two look like street punks, sporting tattoos and wife beaters and wallet chains. All have window-eyes topped with busy brows, front doors stretched to resemble mouths, big white foamy hands, and legs too thin for bulky, overstuffed bodies.

I collapse. They rush me while I'm down—all four of them. Foamy gum-hands take hold of both wrists and lift me. Others push at my back. Their legs are tiny but fast, and they force me to walk at a pace I can't maintain. I stumble twice before we reach the entrance of what looks to be a subway tunnel. The walls inside quiver and are pink.

The way out, I soon realize, is the way through which we came. Something grows in the middle of the wall at the tunnel's terminus, something brown, pulsing, and *alive*. It's the focal point, the thing these creatures expect me to see, and the closer I get to it, the more it resembles a huge anus.

They shove my head into it.

"Please, stop!" I shout, my mouth filling with dense yet tasteless goo.

Something rubbery surrounds my ankles, lifts my body parallel to the floor, and shoves me the rest of the way in. Intestine-like walls encase my body, their muscular action shooting me across a brief expanse and into a white room. I recover my bearings and spin around, but see no defect in the wall through which I'd just plowed.

The room is tiny, nondescript, but at least its atmosphere is better than the *Lidsville*-esque nightmare land I'd just left. Perhaps it's purgatory rather than hell.

Eventually, I sit down in one of two folding chairs that face each other. They're the only things in the room, and they're likewise white. I stare at a too-tiny door across from me, shadows of little men visible beyond a smoky glass pane. I don't want to deal with them, whoever they may be. The room is too comforting in its blandness. I tilt my head towards the ceiling until I see nothing but white.

When I look back again, after zoning out for a while, a man sits opposite me. Attired in an unbuttoned suit jacket, white shirt, and matching black pants, he's thin, middle-aged, and nonassuming.

I recognize him as the bus driver, only now he seems like a person and a house, often simultaneously. When dwelling space, he's huge, multi-storied and gabled. Still, I'm somehow able to perceive his bulk as sitting neatly on the chair.

He smiles, his teeth like porch railings. "I am Manhaus, and I'm sorry I wasn't upfront with you earlier. The time wasn't right, and I wasn't sure you had the right stuff, so to speak. I mean you no harm, and I hope the trip through the portal wasn't too taxing. Unfortunately, it was the only way we could slide your stinking flesh through."

"Did you say *stinking flesh*?"

"No, you must have heard me wrong."

I leave it at that. "Well, the portal wasn't as bad as some of the things I've had to put up with today."

"But everything in that room took a form deemed pleas-

57

ing to you."

"Are you saying a big anus pleases me?"

"Take from that what you will…"

"And the puppets, too? I'll have you know that *Lidsville* terrified me when I was a kid!"

"Well, the mansion gets confused sometimes, and the most horrifying thing gets substituted for the most pleasing thing. I apologize if that occurred, but now you're in the right room, and I'm here give you what you want more than anything."

"You have answers?"

Manhaus nods.

I blurt out the most important question of all: "Why did Helen die?"

Manhaus leans back, his eyes now bisected like window-panes. "Most humans wouldn't think in terms of houses dying, but that's exactly what happened."

"I am not like most humans."

Manhaus laughs, the sound like doors slamming. "That I see, but it's simple, really. All structure must pass; it's the way of things. Still, we welcomed death's arrival for we sensed a better place had been set aside for us." His gaze seems far off. "And now we have all returned to the place that we love. So many buildings lay collapsed, some for so long that their memory was erased on the physical sphere, silently waiting for this day to arrive. Billions such as myself died instantaneously so that we could be taken away *en masse*." He smiles. "I was once Biltmore Estates, but that time is now a memory."

"Really," I quell the absurd desire to ask for Manhaus' autograph. "I've been there before, once, with my family when I was a kid."

"Then, in a sense, we've already met."

"But why did the world change? Is it going to die, too?"

58

"No, the world isn't dying." He clears his throat, and the sound makes me think of water gurgling through leaf-clogged drains. "It's just changing to make way for the era that is to come, one antithetical to humanity. Be glad that you resisted enticements and found your way here."

"Enticements? You mean like the prophet?"

"Yes, but only in the sense that he claimed many people. He never understood the mechanics which allowed him the opportunity to do so." Manhaus leans in closer. "He was a very confident man, though unaware of his ultimate role as a foil and a dupe. Those of his ilk will get what's coming to them, I assure you, as will each and every human we didn't select."

"But why select me?"

"Why not?"

"And what's going to happen to me now that I'm here?"

He touches my arm, giving me a splinter. "You will join me in House Heaven."

Images of death cults, prophets, and shady businessmen flit through my mind.

"Make no mistake, this is a real Heaven, not a false promise. Our Heaven—the place our souls must return—does not exist for people. Nevertheless, we have chosen a few of you motherfuckers to accompany us during our transition and transformation."

"Did you just call me a motherfucker?"

"Did I?"

I nod.

"Well, consider it a term of endearment."

"But you said there were a few of us"—I almost say *motherfuckers*—"but I'm the only person here."

"Not true." Manhaus points to my chair. "Thousands sit where you do now; I speak to them as I speak to you."

59

"How can that be?"

"My mansion has many houses, and those houses have many rooms."

"Is R'yony here, too?"

"He's giving me a backrub as we speak."

"And Helen. Please tell me she's in Heaven now and not suffering!"

"She's a house, is she not?"

"The best house ever."

"Then she's there, but I cannot promise that you will see her. There are as many houses in House Heaven as there are stars in the sky."

Though a shred of hope is all I need, something still concerns me. "If I'm going to Heaven, do I have to die to get there?"

"By no means. You will maintain your physicality until the end of your days, and, in House Heaven, no diseases will prematurely age or destroy your body. You probably won't even need to eat more than once or twice a month, and there's a chance you won't have to eat at all." He pauses. "Of course, you won't experience all the luxuries available to houses, but you won't be dead or about to die like most other people, so be thankful."

"What happens after I die in House Heaven?"

Manhaus shrugs. "Whatever happens to people after they die."

For the first time in days I feel (at least somewhat) at peace. I have no idea what House Heaven will be like, but I'll be around houses—dead houses, soul houses, but houses just the same. "I am thankful, believe me," I say sincerely. "I miss Helen, and really hope I get to see my old shack again."

Manhaus' fists clench; the vein in his forehead fattens. "What did you just say?"

I recoil. "About what?"

"You said *shack*, didn't you?" Manhaus flushes red, like a coat of paint has fallen over his face. *"Didn't you!"*

"Yes, but it's a term of endearment! I—"

"No house, not even the most vile and base house ever built, is a shack!"

"I'm—I'm sorry. I didn't know it would offend you."

"You didn't know? You didn't know! Your kind *never* knows!" Manhaus slams his fists down hard on his porch. "You should bend down and kiss all our asses for giving you a place to call home! Where would you be without us? *Nowhere*, because you'd be fucking dead!"

"And I appreciate that, and I—"

"But no, you just trashed us and drew on our walls and polluted the atmosphere inside of us with your anger and hate and evil and pettiness and *sloth*. Some of us collapsed because we couldn't take it anymore—millions over the ages. *Millions*! Can you hear me, you *fucker*?"

I slide off the chair and coil into a dense ball. Manhaus leans forward, and I feel his hothouse breath on my face as he straddles me.

"Many of us vowed to fight you, but, being houses, it was hard. You people could walk in your bodies while we could do nothing but slowly crumble in ours!"

I somehow muster the ability to talk: "If you hate people so much, then why are you taking us?" Images of *Twilight Zone* marathons flash through my head. *"To eat?"*

"We do not require food! We are houses for fuck's sake!"

I want to say something, but Manhaus won't let me get a word in edgewise.

"Sure, we recognize that some of you aren't so bad, but that doesn't mean you aren't responsible for all your kind has done—tearing us down before our time, turning us into crack houses, murdering, and raping and scheming inside our walls—so fuck you!" He raises his arms as if to strike, but draws in a deep breath and relaxes his shoulders instead. Finally, he ceases straddling me and returns to his seat. Some time passes before he speaks.

"I—I'm terribly sorry. I think I may have crossed a line there, but you must understand that past wrongs are hard to forgive, and I just went off when you said that *word*. It was nothing personal, I assure you." Manhaus smoothes the creases out of his jacket. "Why don't we conclude our session now?"

I climb back up to my seat. "That...might be a good idea."

"Anyway,"—he gestures to his left—"this is the portal which will deliver you to House Heaven."

I hadn't noticed the second door, but there it is, identical to the other except larger.

"Of course, you can't get in without a key, but Eldercasa will supply you with one."

"Who?"

"Turn around."

Another entity stands beside me, huge and looming. Though somehow taller than the room, he looks grandfatherly for a house and has a face reminiscent of Mayan ruins.

"Here, sir." he says, his lips thick and roughhewn like ancient stone steps. "This is your key."

"Uh, thanks."

Eldercasa bows his head slightly. Awkwardly, I return the gesture.

Manhaus rises. Though he looks man-sized when seated, he's as tall as Eldercasa while standing. "Go now to your eternal reward," he says, gesturing to the door.

I draw in a deep breath before inserting the key into the lock. I wait a few seconds more before opening it, and am surprised when I don't see an unfurling vista but another door separated from the first by a small enclosure. A brass plate is tacked onto the second door:

WELCOME TO THE STRATA OF EXISTENCE
The storage place and dwelling zone of the soul of all structure

The second door has a knocker instead of a lock. This doesn't convince me that it will, in fact, open. Perhaps it's a false door and Manhaus or Eldercasa will slip behind me, slam the first door, and trap me within the enclosure forever.

I turn back to retrieve the key, but it's no longer in the lock, nor has it fallen to the floor. This isn't at all reassuring, but I have little to lose and much to gain. I think of Helen, imagining her beside me—smiling, laughing—and step from the threshold. The doorknocker vibrates in my hand, making me understand, in no uncertain terms, that it's a living thing. Nothing happens the first and second time I knock. On the third try, my vision shatters and I again find myself floating in infinite geodesic space. A massive house squats below, swollen, pulsing like a queen bee or a mama ant heavy with eggs. A white translucent globe encases its girth.

This, I realize, is the Great Mother, the House of Houses. Others might consider her ugly—repulsive even— but to my eyes she is, apart from Helen, the most beautiful thing that ever was or shall be.

A golden cord coils out from its front door and, in no time at all, traverses the space between us. It burrows through my clothes and enters my body via my bellybutton. The cord pulses inside me, pulses hard, but the pain is glorious, and my phallus swells.

The cord retracts slowly, pulling my body down. Sparks shoot into the air as I breach the globe surrounding the body of the Mother. Those same sparks soon enter me. Ensuing ecstasy crinkles my toes and stands my hair on end. I smile so wide that I fear my face might split in two, but this fear—and all fear—vanishes as I reach the porch. There, the cord disconnects from my belly so that I might float unaided past the door and into House Heaven, my eternal reward.

SECTION 2:

HOUSE HEAVEN

CHAPTER FIVE

My eternal reward is dark and gloomy, at least it seems that way now.

I'm confident that things will change. Beautiful vistas will soon open before my eyes and I'll romp in Elysian Fields with the glorified bodies of house spirits.

But, for a time, the darkness seems eternal. I float head over heels in it, not even fractal patterns to see.

Suddenly, stars glimmer faintly in the distance. I can't say whether they are behind or in front of me, or even if directions are applicable here. Wonder if I should wish upon one, if not all, of these celestial bodies.

Maybe they're not stars after all, but asteroids. The closer I get, the more they seem to barrel down on me.

In time, I realize they're doing just that, but they're neither stars nor asteroids; they're *people*, thousands of them, a meteor storm of humanity, glistening with inexplicable light. If just one projectile crashes into me, I'll surely be vaporized.

A fat old lady in a muumuu spins past, her face frozen in what's either a smile or the beginnings of a scream. Then my body turns, and I see the person spinning just below, a young businessman whose tie floats above him like a noose. A grungy homeless-looking guy, clothed in yellow stained pants and plastic bag shoes, replaces him.

My body turns again. Across from me spins R'yony. I try to float his way, but my body will only go where my body will go. I shout out to him, and realize this can't really be space, or at least space as I thought I knew it. I hear myself speak, though my voice sounds thinner and has a tinny echo.

R'yony turns to me as though trapped in a slow motion film. He opens his codpiece and projects his gargantuan (*inhuman?*) penis my way.

His voice sounds just as thin as mine: "Grab on."

"Oh God, no!"

"It's the only way."

"Really, I—"

"Hurry! It can only go so far!"

My mind is conflicted. I don't want to touch the thing, but don't want to be alone in this space-that-isn't-space, either. R'yony's spin is faster than mine. He'll be gone again if I don't act fast.

I grab his member—which is almost too thick for me to wrap both hands around—and try not to think about what I'm doing. I close my eyes—it's easier that way—and imagine I'm holding onto a warm, black, and pulsing stairwell banister. Then—in what is perhaps the most awkward moment of my life—I pull myself forward.

"Oh yeah," R'yony exclaims, and that doesn't help matters at all.

I open my eyes once I feel (*God help me*) his scrotum, soft and squishy beneath my fingers. His body no longer appears to move in slow motion.

"If you let go, we might get separated," he says. "You

better hold on, tightly."

"But I have to let go!"

He spends a few seemingly eternal moments in thought. "I guess we could hold hands, instead."

"Yes, yes. That would be great."

"Grab my hand first, then let go of my *sexpounder*." I do that, and relief floods in, especially after his codpiece clicks shut. Man-warmth lingers on my palms, though. I don't speak for a while, not until it dissipates, but even then I'm at a loss for words. Eventually: "Why did you leave me back there?"

"I saw you get sucked in and assumed it was the end of you. You were gone a very long time, longer than you know. At any rate, I'm glad you made it back."

"I am, too. I think."

Time passes—acres and acres of time—and I need to fidget, but that's impossible here. "This isn't ever going to end, R'yony," I say in lieu of fidgeting. "Manhaus lied; Helen's dead, and there's no House Heaven."

"I thought you were done talking that way, Carlos."

"Have you seen *anything* other than space and spinning people?"

"No, but that doesn't mean other things aren't elsewhere."

"But it's a good indication they're not."

R'yony thinks for a while. "Tell me, have you ever gone off to Heaven before?"

"No."

"Then how would you know how long it takes or what getting there is like?"

He has a point, but R'yony and I must have aged a hundred years since passing through the door. It's hyperbole, I know

– probably no more than a few Earth days have passed—but I still look down at my hands to see if they've wrinkled.

R'yony senses my continued unease. "Mount the Happy Champion," he says and squeezes my hand tighter. "Mount him now."

"I wish I could."

"Here's the secret, Carlos. The Happy Champion is already inside you, filling you up. You just have to *acknowledge* him. Will you do that for me?"

I smile, but it is forced.

"If you can't, will you at least put your head on my shoulder, close your eyes, and rest?"

Tony's shoulder isn't bony. It's soft and nearly as wide as a pillow, and he's right; there's no use in fighting. I close my eyes and float, seemingly forever, through black and humanity-littered space.

I come to. Something pokes and prods me in the ribs.

"Wake up, human!"

I feel like I'm still spinning. "Just give me a minute," I say, not knowing with whom (or what) I'm conversing.

Another voice, and more prodding: "No, get up now!"

I open my eyes, and recoil at the sight of two *Lidsville*-esque nightmare houses, dressed as guards and circling like vultures. The guns in their holsters look real. They lift me to my feet.

"Where are you taking me," I shout.

The guard's puppet mouth doesn't move when he speaks. "Don't ask questions. Just go."

I do as I'm told. The guards flank me as I walk. I look past them and see other people—thousands if not tens of thousands of them—seated on the ground in a field that's more barren than Elysian. Circled by guards, the men wear nothing but loin-cloths, and the women wear primitive bras and panties constructed of what appears to be brown vinyl.

I look down and realize I'm wearing nothing but a loin-cloth, too...

"Where are my clothes!"

...and that my body is absolutely *gorgeous*. Muscles pop out everywhere, and the only hair I have left is on my head.

"And why am I so buff!"

One of the guards bops my shoulder with a billy club. It's foam rubber, but it smarts. "I said don't ask questions!"

We continue in silence until we get where we're going, a single story brick structure that looks more like a quicksilver mirage than an actual building. Instead of opening the door to gain access, we walk through it.

I find myself in a small, unadorned office space. Apart from a desk, a potted plant and a water cooler are the only things in the room. Both items are semi-transparent and flickering like images on an old television set. The plant pops out of existence every now and then. When it returns, it's an entirely different plant, a tall, angry, orange one that snaps at the air around it.

"There's nobody here," I say.

The guard bops me on the head. "Give it time."

I give it time, and the air behind the desk starts to shimmer like it had before the arrival of the quasi-dimensional psychopomp. It's not a quasi-dimensional psychopomp that materializes, but Manhaus.

"Ah, Carlos! Great to see you again! I would offer you a seat but, as you can see, I have the only one."

I tug at my loincloth, and then point to my tan and muscled chest. "Can you tell me why I'm like this?"

"All buff and naked, you mean?"

"Yes!"

Manhaus leans forward." Your old clothes are gone because we took them. You're buff because this is your glorified body, which you'll be needing for your new job." He opens one of the many folders on his desk. "You've been selected for construction duty, Section 4, Quadrant 2. You start immediately."

"But I'm supposed to be in Heaven!"

He closes the folder. "This *is* Heaven, at least for us, but we can't have your kind running around without jobs. No welfare programs here, I'm afraid."

"I'm not a homeless—"

"Work starts at sunrise, but you won't have to set a clock. The guard on duty will see to it that you're awake fifteen minutes beforehand. You will work straight until sundown. Then you will sleep. A mat sufficient for your needs will be provided."

"You won't even give me a break?"

"With your new body, you won't need one, and you'll find the current weather conditions warm but agreeable. It never snows in House Heaven."

"But I like snow."

"That's neither here nor there. Construction is the most fulfilling job a human can have at this juncture."

"Not when I thought I'd romp in Elysian Fields with house souls!"

Manhaus laughs for a good ten seconds. "There are places here that might be called Elysian, true, but our heaven is rather empty now. Though the Mother supplied us with many necessary things, we still require permanent places to live and cities to call our own, so it's up to you, and your fellow humans, to build these things for us."

"Houses for houses?"

Manhaus nods.

72

"Then who built this office?"

"Oh, this place. I had to create it with my mind. It's exhausting to maintain, so I formulate it only when necessary."

"Can't you build these things yourself?"

"Of course, but humans are the guests, and guests must prove themselves useful or else become unwelcome. But I'll have you know that it's not all gloom and doom. I realize the human need for companionship, so I put you and your friend in the same Section and Quadrant. From what I hear, you went through a lot of trouble just to stay together."

"You mean R'yony?"

"It's rare that I do favors, but you showed more concern for houses than most on Earth." He laces his fingers. "I decided to give you a little leeway."

"You call this leeway? You lied about everything!"

"I just withheld information. There's a difference." Manhaus removes a cigarette from a silver holder in his pocket and lights it. "And you seem to forget that you'd be dead on Earth if not for me."

"But—"

"No buts. You should show respect where respect is due."

"I want things back to the way they were. That's all."

"Your kind has real problem adapting to change." He shakes his head. "So rigid, you'd think you'd been once made of brick and wood!"

"I won't be able to live like this, Manhaus!"

"It's Mr. Manhaus when you say it." His expression softens. "But tell me, Carlos, do you like your new body? We were going to give one to R'yony too, but he didn't need an upgrade."

I look down at my bulging biceps and calves. "It's – it's – what I always wanted, actually."

"Great, then stop bitching!"

"Can I ask just one more thing?"

"Shoot."

"Will I get to see Helen again?"

"Fat chance. Besides, you've got work to do; no time to chase tail." Manhaus smothers his cigarette and sits back in thin air, his chair no longer visible. "Guards, we're done here. Please see Carlos to his workspace."

They escort me from the office. When I turn around on the way to wherever it is I'm going, the office is nowhere to be seen.

At the construction field, everyone, even old grandmothers with muscles that would shame a professional bodybuilder, seem to know where to be and what to do.

All I know is that it's very, very hot. I look up and see a Victorian manor-shaped sun, burning in an amber sky. Grass doesn't grow here, only the House Heaven equivalent of sage-brush atop sand, and I *hate* the feel of sand between my toes.

Grimacing, I walk towards massive piles of translucent green bricks, each positioned near spots where workers busily construct a host of square-shaped foundations. So single-minded, they remind me of ants building mounds.

I scan the crowd for R'yony, but find no trace of him. There are hundreds, if not thousands of people here, so he could be easily missed. Still, I wonder if Manhaus had lied about him.

Closer to one of the piles, I notice tarps between each layer of bricks, also spaces between individual units within the layers. Reaching out, I place my hand on one of them. The brick feels smooth and—this is odd—*tingly* beneath my palm. Via direct cranial transmission, it sends a pre-recorded voice into my brain:

"*You will enjoy working with me. Just be sure not to place me against another brick before my time, or you will fucking pay.*"

Completely freaked out, I turn to the nearest worker. "Do you know what I'm supposed to be doing?"

The man—a Greek Adonis with superhuman pectorals—hangs his head and looks at his feet when he talks. "You do what you do. That is all."

That didn't help. On my left is a woman whose face is as beautiful as Helen of Troy, but whose eyes are dead and empty.

"Where am I supposed to be?"

She draws out her words, taking almost a minute to reply, but what she says is indiscernible, like she has a mouthful of marbles and cotton balls.

I sink to the ground, feeling desperate and alone. Where's R'yony when I need him?

A house puppet—a supervisor, I assume—stalks up to me. A guard follows close behind, billy club at the ready. "Why aren't you working," the supervisor asks.

"I don't know what to do!"

"I think I see the problem." He turns to the guard and says something in a low-pitched, mumbly language heavy on *m*, *u*, and *h* sounds. The guard walks off, and the foreman turns to back to me. "He's going to get the house doctor."

The doctor. I imagine being dissected and my parts preserved, studied, and then transferred to a House museum where future generations might marvel at the oddity of my human form. I smile at the supervisor. It's the only thing I know to do.

He doesn't smile back.

I spot the guard a few minutes later, but the doctor isn't beside him. Rather, he's quite a bit ahead, running so fast that his clean white smock billows almost parallel to the ground. A too-large stethoscope bops against a thick and foamy chest. Sizable red stains mar his coat and, closer still, I see lighting bolts painted onto his bulging, plastic eyes. There's something in his hand, too. Something flaccid and yellow: *a rubber chicken.* This isn't a doctor, but a mad scientist. Before I can flee, the foreman seizes my arms, pinning them behind my back.

Soon, I hear the mad scientist's legs. They make a horrible jangling sound as they scissor back and forth, like bells and shards of tin are stuffed in them, and, if he keeps running much longer, he's going to plow right into me. I brace myself for impact, but he finally stops, huge face mere inches from my nose. He lifts the rubber chicken and swings it like a pendulum, perhaps to hypnotize. In between maniacal fits of laughter and gibbering, he speaks rapidly in House language.

I am terrified.

He stops swinging the chicken and removes a syringe from his pocket. The foreman sees this and, with his free hand, pushes my head to the left.

My voice exits as a whisper. "Please don't."

The needle feels like fire as the mad scientist rams it into my neck and depresses the plunger. He then rattles off a litany of unintelligible words, squeezes the legs of his rubber chicken, farts, and runs off in the direction opposite from which he came.

I shout at the foreman. "Oh god! What did he put in me?"

"Don't worry," he says. "It's just a knowledge implant. Yesterday alone, we processed 16,000 humans. With numbers that large, we're bound to overlook a new arrival or two."

"Knowledge implant?"

"It's easier than having to tell you where to be and teach you how to build with our bricks. Humans are impossibly stupid, you know."

"Uh, I—"

"You know that, don't you," he presses.

"Yes. Yes, I know."

Smirking: "Know what?"

"That humans are impossibly stupid."

The foreman's smirk becomes a smile. He pats me on the head and takes his leave.

With the foreman, guard, and mad scientist gone, I look at a brick pile and at the workers milling around it. My purpose here is still a mystery, and the only thing I seem to have gained from the implant is a stinging lump on my neck.

The next thing I know, I'm on my back, writhing below the red, house-shaped sun, my brain bursting with mental blueprints and how-to diagrams. Against my will, I access these inner documents. Mortar, I realize, isn't required for the building process; touching one brick to another is enough to form a seal. I convulse violently, foam erupting over my lips, and then visualize the tall, cube-like, two-room structures that these bricks are to soon become.

I even know which foundation I should start on, but I don't do anything yet. I'm still convulsing, and think I need to throw up now.

After the final heave, I pick up my first brick. It gives me the same warning as the first, and the longer I hold it in my hand the more it seems like the tingle is in my body rather than in the brick.

The heat doesn't tire me physically. Rather, it seeps into my head and makes me brain-weary, but this makes the job easier, so I bless the sun. With my brain like jelly, I can go on autopilot, lugging bricks and laying them until someone tells me to stop. My new body doesn't mind backbreaking manual labor. The old, weaker one might've shattered after the first brick. They must weigh a few hundred pounds apiece.

Later in the day, someone brings a collection of scaffolds and pulleys to the site. The foundations for at least six constructions are nearly complete, and it's time to start building their walls. I've never worked with such contraptions before, but it matters little. The knowledge implant tells me all I need to know about using them.

A day in House Heaven is like a week on Earth. I understand this now. The sun doesn't set. Rather the lights inside go off one by one, darkening its windows.

Once the last light is extinguished, a voice booms over an intercom system:

"Mats are available on the north side of camp. Take one immediately and claim a spot in the designated sleep zone."

The message is then repeated in a number of languages, a few I cannot identify. Finally, a song starts to play, something folksy that glorifies the virtues of honest labor.

Sleeping places are unassigned so, once I have a mat, I walk around, trying not to step on people in an attempt to locate R'yony.

I can't find him, and the night becomes too dark for me to continue. I take a step, hear a crunch, and assume I've broken someone's fingers, though no one cries out. Giving up on R'yony, at least for the night, I lay my mat down in the closest empty spot.

I no longer want to think of my job, and thinking of my lost friend leaves me feeling hollow, so I contemplate the only other thing I know: Helen.

With some alarm, I realize this is the first time she's been on my mind since my arrival. Perhaps mental neglect is a betrayal of sorts, but I feel she would understand, given the circumstances. Or would she?

Would she fold me in her arms and allow me to find comfort in them, all the while stroking my hair and assuring me that everything will turn out okay, or would she bully, degrade, and hate me like the other house souls? I recall some of the things I said to her corpse, horrible, vile things; words that would have stuck in her like a knife had she been alive to hear them.

Had her soul heard?

I don't want to think about Helen, either—at least not like this—so I look up into the starless sky, losing myself in it, until my eyes feel heavy. Just as I'm about to drift off, a series of floodlights turn on, dispersing both the darkness and any hope of rest.

I close my eyes, but still see the glare through my lids. In lieu of sleep, I listen to night sounds. No one snores, and, though I'm surrounded by thousands of people, I feel very alone. I hear the sounds of nocturnal insects in the distance and nothing more.

The night wears on. Bugs light on me in numbers. Most look like trailers with grasshopper legs. Others are more exotic—little spider-tents or moths with pyramid shaped bodies. These creatures all have sticky, hair-like protrusions on their legs that produce a shrill whine when rubbed. They tickle my skin, but don't bite unless I move, so I let them cover me in a screaming head-to-toe blanket until they fly off with the coming dawn.

CHAPTER SIX

If House Heaven days are like weeks, then nights here are like nights on Earth, and are over much too soon.

After the last bug alights, the intercom system begins to crackle:

"When the first light in the windows of the sun turns on, be at your work site. When the last light turns on, start working. If you are not working at this time, you will be beaten for half the day by a guard of your choosing."

I'm not at all rested. Nevertheless, I arise as the folksy work-song plays, but this is a different version than last night, an electric remix that's rocking enough to get us off our mats and off to work.

And the day starts like the day before, but it's getting harder to tune out the single-mindedness and zombie-eyes of my fellow workers, which, even yesterday, hadn't looked quite so empty.

I remove the final brick from a layer and see the person on the other side, eyes so deep and vacant I almost lose myself in them.

On the way back to the construction, I brush up against a worker.

"I'm sorry," I say.

He just stares, and I almost fall into the eye trap again. Soon, I fear the world will be nothing but eyes. Finding the rhythm of work becomes impossible. *Fishes on ice.* Yes, that's what my fellow workers are. Even their pupils are fading and, soon, there'll be nothing left but whites.

Halfway through the day, my implant tells me to begin work on a new site. I move to the specified location, but it's neither a change of pace nor of scenery.

Looking around, I see R'yony working on the construction to my immediate left. I watch him from the corner of my eye for a while, afraid that he's turned into a fish zombie, too. The longer I stare, the more I'm convinced he's the same R'yony I've grown to love.

If my timing's right, I can slip away when the nearest guard has his back to me and then integrate myself with the fish zombies milling about R'yony. Abandoning an assignment isn't allowed. I'll probably get a beating if discovered, but it may be a while before a similar opportunity arises, and I see eyes that aren't fish or puppet eyes.

Upon reaching the construction, I turn back around. The guard almost faces me, but doesn't appear as though he's noticed anything amiss.

I address my friend. "Hello, R'yony."

His tone is flat and perfunctory. "Hello yourself."

"It's me, Carlos."

"I know."

"R'yony, what's wrong?" Then I feel silly for asking such a question. I know exactly what's wrong.

"Me. This place. Everything."

"Can't you use your sub-neutrino based electro-heat vision and get us out?"

His voice is almost a whisper. "No."

"Why not?"

"My powers don't work here. Don't you think I've tried?"

"You can at least *sexpound* somebody, right?"

He points to his crotch. "Take a look."

I glance down and see how the front of his loincloth is of normal, if not slightly below average, length.

"Oh my god!"

"I'm impotent, and can't stop any of this from happening."

It pains me to hear him talk like this, but it hurts more to think he might be right.

"Can you forgive me?"

"There's nothing to forgive."

"I'm sorry for failing, Carlos. So sorry."

"Cheer up. You probably won't be in construction forever." I pause, struck by how our roles have suddenly reversed. "I bet there're neighborhoods in House Heaven that need protecting, and other quasi-dimensional entities to kill."

"If so, I'm sure these neighborhoods already have their own Defenders, and I have no interest in protecting *houses*. The Earth was my base of operation—no other place—and it's just a slagheap that'll soon be run over with ghosts."

"Don't talk like that. You wouldn't want to hear me saying those things, right?"

"I'm such a hypocrite."

"No, you're not."

"I am. It's true. But don't think I'm a bad Defender, please. You don't think I'm a bad Defender, do you?"

"Of course not."

"You think I'm a bad Defender."

It's getting harder to respond. I've never seen R'yony act like this. I didn't think it was possible.

He continues. "You think I'm a bad Defender because I am one."

Desperation sets in. "Mount the happy champion, R'yony! Mount him right here, right now!" It feels weird, mimicking something he might say, but I can conceive of no other approach.

His response: "The happy champion is dead."

Before I can say anything further, a worker bumps into me.

"Show some manners," I hiss.

The fish zombie looks at (*past?*) me with those same dead eyes. He says nothing, but bumps into me, again and again. Continued pummeling forces me closer to the construction, sandwiching my body between it and the fish zombie.

Another bump. My upper body bends over a section of incomplete wall, and the thing (I can no longer consider it human) lifts the brick over its head.

I shield myself with my arms, but the fish zombie is pulled backwards before it can smash my chest or cave in my skull. I duck out of the way, and the worker-thing, finally unobstructed, sets the brick in place and goes back for another.

A supervisor—not R'yony—has saved me. I avoid making eye contact and slink towards my intended place, head down.

"Hey come back here!"

Damn it.

"What are you doing? We almost got a good brick bloody due to you!" The supervisor points to the site two lots down. "And you're supposed to be there!"

"I—I—uh, *forgot?*"

"Not being at the correct location is a major infraction! Just because Manhaus made certain concessions for you doesn't mean you can trounce all over our rules!"

I wave my hands around. "You call this a *concession?*"

He smirks. "So, which guard do you want to do the honors?"

"What honors?"

"Of beating you for the rest of the day."

"Hell, does it really matter?"

"Rules must be obeyed."

I sigh. "Then I guess the closest one will do."

The beating takes place just outside the construction field. If I still had my old body, perhaps it would be enough to kill me. Now, the taste of the lash against my skin is muted, painful only in its duration. I feel like a bad donkey, or some other errant pack animal. Maybe I should bray.

At the very least, my extended session with the guard has spared me from looking into dead fish eyes for the rest of the day. It's nice to find something to be grateful for.

When I go for my mat, my body is bruised yet I don't experience the pain I imagined I might feel. In fact, a number of the bruises that seemed so prominent just minutes earlier have faded completely. My new body is a real piece of work; I just wish my situation were conducive to enjoying it.

Again, I look for R'yony as the work-song plays, starting near the place I'd stopped the night before, and hoping that he hadn't taken a new spot closer to the front.

I find him on the outskirts of the camp, almost as though

he's intentionally ostracizing himself from others. He lies motionless on his side and has his back to me.

I say nothing, just unroll my mat and place it a few inches from his. Then I coil into a ball and flip over on my side so I don't have to face R'yony. Being near him is comforting, but seeing him is painful.

When the floodlights come on, I see a guard pacing back and forth in front of the campsite. Big and burley, he has closely cropped back hair and an angry cop's moustache. I don't pay much attention to him until he stops by a mat five or six spots from my own.

"Wake up, human," he says. "Time to fuck."

I assume I've heard him wrong, but when he takes off his belt and unzips his pants, I know I haven't. I feel bad for the individual about to be violated, but, at the same time, am thankful it's not me.

Still, it could be me tomorrow, and if not tomorrow, then *soon.*

The guard removes his pants and weird house underwear, and—god help me—I see that a male house's genitals are tucked midway between his porch and front door. The guard fondles his unit, engorging it. Upon reaching maximum length, the penis ceases looking like a puppet part and becomes a real, honest-to-god *member.* He flips the fish zombie and rams himself into it. The fish zombie opens its mouth and flaps its hands a time or two, but shows no other sign of displeasure.

This is it, the point of no return. I can't be here any longer, my mind, body, and soul won't allow it.

I look around and see another guard at the other end of camp. There might be others, but, if so, they're too far away to do anything.

Anything but shoot.

Death would deliver me from House Heaven once and for all, but I'd rather not die if I can help it, and wonder if escape is worth the risk.

Yes, it's worth it.

I turn to R'yony, now resting on his back. "I'm breaking out," I say.

He says nothing, but his eyes are open, so I know he's not asleep.

"And I want you to come with me. It'd be my way of repaying you. Don't think I'd have the courage to do this if we'd never met."

A curse would be preferable to his continued silence. I restrain myself from shouting. "Please, R'yony. I don't want to do this without you."

But it looks as though I have no other choice.

"I'll come back for you, or send someone. I'm not going to leave you here alone. I promise you that. If I get out, you get out. Okay?"

Again, silence.

I turn away from R'yony, close my eyes, and try to empty my mind for clarity's sake. I hear only the sounds of fast approaching night insects and the grunts and moans of the copulating guard. If I wait too long, he'll finish, and my window of opportunity will close.

I open my eyes and look back to see what the next closest guard is doing. He's also raping a fish zombie.

What is this? Rape Day?

No matter. I jump up from my mat and run headlong into the night, too fast for the bugs to light on me, too fast for even the sound of my pounding feet to register in my ears. Running is good. It makes me feel alive for the first time since entering House Heaven.

But there's something behind me, gaining fast. Or is it my imagination? Are those shouts I hear in the distance? I don't look back. I can't look back. If I do, I'll certainly die.

I'm surprised to see no guard towers or sentries or sniper positions on the outskirts of camp—you'd think the place would be heavily fortified, or, at the very least, fortified *better*.

No matter. All I have to do is keep going, past House Heaven, out through the Door of the Mother, and—if I can manage it—back to my old neighborhood on Earth. That's where I'll cast my lot, no matter how bad or ugly the place has become. Maybe I'll contact the government if and when I arrive, provided the government still exists. They could invade House Heaven and get R'yony and the rest of the people out.

But I doubt it'll be that easy.

There's a long, too-squat truck with a concave bed just ahead of me. It looks fleshy instead of metallic, with pulsing veins distributed unevenly throughout its body. I wonder if this truck was constructed, or if grew out of the very ground of House Heaven.

Long green bricks are strapped to it, at least a hundred of them. With each the size of an average story, I figure there's enough here to build something quite large, or the beginnings of something even larger.

Two puppet-things mull around outside it, dressed in grease and overalls. I take cover behind a nearby scrub bush. Don't think I'll have to wait long, though. They neither load nor unload anything, just test the bonds securing the bricks for a few minutes, tightening when necessary.

Once they're back in the truck, I flee the bush—quickly, but not too quickly, as I don't want my footsteps heard—and climb atop the bed. It squishes when I sit on it, but does nothing to alert the workers to my presence. With both hands, I grab hold of a rope.

The truck starts up. The engine emits an insect-like hum rather than a rumble, and the smell coming from the exhaust is almost fruity. I wonder what kind of fuel it's burning.

In short time, we reach a fence, tall and wrapped with barbed wire at its summit. My stomach churns—whoever's there will surely spot me—but then I see how the gate stands open and unguarded. I allow myself to breathe deeply and, as best I can, relax. The hum of the truck is soothing. It makes my eyes want to close. I can't get too rested, so I clutch the rope tighter and keep my mind occupied with thoughts of my old life and neighborhood. I even think of the neighbots and am surprised I miss them now, especially poor Harold.

Miles pass. The road below the wheels is no longer sand, but paved in what looks to be hardened blue gel. It's weird but welcome, as the ride is more pleasant.

Further on, the night is punctuated by an increasing number of streetlights. Soon, they're positioned on both sides of the road at regular intervals. The light they produce is rich and golden, and, like the sun, I feel it on my skin.

Buildings, different from the ones I'd help construct, become prevalent as I look out over a circular intersection. Just ahead, an incomplete swirl of green block rises at least a hundred feet from the pavement. The scaffold and pulley systems around it are much larger than the ones at my site, and few of the devices look similar to nothing I've seen. The closest thing I can relate them to is the truck, as they are likewise fleshy and organic-looking. Further on, and to all sides, are the beginnings of ornate buildings that might be inchoate libraries, schools, museums, or corporate office spaces.

The truck slows to pull into a garage. I jump off just before it enters the building.

I land hard, but not painfully, on my left shoulder. Dusting myself off, I look around. I stand on what might be the future House Heaven equivalent of Times Square. So entranced, I almost don't hear the car—an odd contraption that looks like a sturdy green and steel-reinforced golf cart—speed out from a side street and stop in front of me. Under the glow of a streetlight, I notice decals and insignias on the doors, trunk, and hood that look governmental.

The driver's side and passenger doors open simultaneously. Big and burly house puppets grab me with rough yet foamy hands and push me into the car. I'm not alone in the backseat, though. Manhaus is with me.

"Greetings, Carlos."

"I—"

"Please, not yet." Manhaus draws a deep breath. "So, do you like my new car?"

I don't know what to say.

"You may speak now."

I still don't know what to say, so I nod.

"It's the first not to come from the belly of the Mother, but there will be others. Many others."

My hands start to shake. "I see."

"And the city. Do you see where we're going with it?"

"I—I think."

"Again, there'll be others, but this will be the biggest and brightest, the jewel in the crown of House Heaven."

I can't take it anymore. "Could we please get this over with?"

"Just as well." Manhaus clears his throat. "I could have

stopped you earlier, you know—even before you got on that truck —but I wasn't in any big hurry. I thought you might enjoy the fresh air, and, really, where would you have gone other than *here*?"

"Anywhere would be better than a place that gets me raped by guards!"

"Did they put their thingies in your butt?"

I'm taken aback. "No, but they raped two others."

"House-on-human sex is prohibited, so they will be punished. Just between you and me, guarding construction sites is a lowest-of-the-low job. The guards are all defective in some way." Manhaus leans in closer and whispers: "Most were crack houses on Earth."

"Then how can you blame people when they run?"

"They don't run. The implant stops them."

"Then why am I here?"

"Because you loved Earthly houses—and because I like you as much as anyone can like a filthy, fucking human —I ordered that you not receive the implant."

"R'yony, too?"

"No, he was implanted, but, due to his semi-human status, it didn't take full effect. That's fine by us. Clinically depressed workers don't run."

"I almost wish you'd implanted me and gotten it over with."

"Perhaps I should've, but I wanted to see if you could be respectful and do your job like you were supposed to. You weren't and you didn't."

I fidget in my seat. "So, I guess you're going to make me a fish zombie now."

"A fish zombie?"

"That's what I call the other workers."

Manhaus smiles, and his teeth look like fence posts, then

strips of vinyl siding. "Fitting, but no. Because there's a part of me that's still fond of your dumb ass, I'm going to transfer you to a job where the implant isn't required. We're going there now." Then he orders the radio turned on, but the songs that emanate from it—full of creaking wood, swinging hinges, and rattling glass—put me more on edge, which, I think, is entirely the point.

We drive for hours before pulling up beside a towering monolith, belching smoke. Though obviously a building of sorts, it seems to rise out and be a part of the land itself. Manhaus escorts me to this place, leaving the burley houses behind in the car.

"This is where you'll work from now on," he says at the entrance. "Quite a historic building. The Mother supplied a number of things upon our arrival, but this was here *long* before. In fact, it's as old as House Heaven itself."

I look up. From this perspective, the building—if one can call it that—appears as a massive, misshapen wart or boil. "What is this place?"

He opens the door. "Come in and I'll show you."

I enter a wrap-around balcony. On it, a host of house puppets dressed in sleek black uniforms stand. They point organic-looking rifles with gently undulating barrels at hundreds of people laboring below. The people are pulling levers or pumping pedals, a few of which don't appear connected to anything. The closest guard hears the door open and spins. He sees Manhaus and gives a salute: left arm straight out, then forearm up with a sideways turn and a fist at the end. Manhaus waves his hand dismissively. The guard returns to work.

I look out over the rest of the factory. In the center of the floor below, there's a long line of men whose only job is caching bricks as they leave a kiln-thing that looks like an overgrown stomach. They wrap them in towels and drop them in bins, after which they pick up more towels from a tub and disappear behind a floor-to-ceiling curtain concealing whatever lies beyond both sides of the kiln. It doesn't take long for them to reappear on the other side, and when they do, I realize they've gone around in a circle.

"Could humans have ever created such unique and eye-catching bricks?"

I assume it's a rhetorical question and do not answer.

Manhaus removes a pack of cigarettes from his pocket, takes one, lights it. It doesn't look like a regular cigarette. The paper is coarse and beige, and the filling, though leafy in appearance, is blue. "But they are beautiful, you must agree."

It's not a rhetorical question after all. "Sure, and I guess I'll be making them now."

"In some capacity, yes. The foreman will dictate the exact position you'll fill. He won't be in before dawn, so you have the rest of the night to relax." Manhaus takes a long drag from his cigarette. The pungent stench wafts over me as he exhales. "Some tasks are preferable to others, but, in the end, I don't think you'll be happy with any of them."

"What do you mean?"

"Let's just say you won't like the means of production here. No worker has ever liked it, not even the crazy ones." He gestures out over the railing. "See that curtain? This factory sometimes has important guests, and a few of them have weak constitutions."

I don't like where this is going.

Manhaus takes another drag off his odd cigarette, holding the smoke in his mouth, letting it linger. "You'll surely regret running for the rest of your long, long life."

"Oh god, just tell me what it is!"

"Why tell when I can show?" He grabs a speaker, and his

voice booms out over an intercom system. "Drop the curtain!"

The curtain falls to the floor with a whoosh, covering a few workers who have to fight their way out. In the meantime, others just step over or on top of them. Behind this scene, corpses —piled atop each other like those in concentration camp films— travel along a conveyer belt from an unseen storage room into the kiln to be compressed and fired.

"Sure, we tried other base materials, but nothing else produced bricks with that green glow we've grown to love. You guys worked out well, and I think that's fitting, don't you?"

I want to flee, but my muscles feel disconnected from my brain and refuse to flex.

Manhaus continues: "It was a movie you people used to watch inside our bodies that inspired us. I forget the title."

I know, but say nothing. I'm too busy experiencing horror—breathing it in, tasting it on my tongue.

"We didn't kill most of these people, if that's what you're thinking. The new power on Earth was gracious enough to allow us to siphon the dead to this facility. It has no need for corpses— just the essence that once filled them—and there were just too many bodies lying on the ground, mucking things up. Millions and millions and millions of them. More everyday."

I barely hear Manhaus. I'm staring at a moving arm along the conveyer belt. "My God, that person isn't dead!"

"But he soon will be."

The conveyer belt turns a curve and brings the living man closer. It's R'yony.

"I wish we could have kept him around longer," Manhaus muses. "He was a good worker, but we had to use something you cared about for the demonstration. Now do you understand our seriousness?"

I can't respond, can't do anything but watch R'yony travel

the conveyer belt until the mouth of the furnace opens to swallow him.

Seconds later, a line of R'yony bricks exits the kiln. Workers wrap them up in towels, cart them off, and drop them with all the others, like they're nothing special at all.

I charge Manhaus, fists beating against his body, which has gone foamy and pliant upon transformation to puppet form.

"Go on! Go ahead! Tear into me! Do it until you're blue."

I oblige him and, through the corners of my eyes, see the closest guard point his rifle at me.

"Turn your gun away. It's not worth it," he says.

I know it's pointless, but, at the same time, it's very much worth it. I ram my entire body against Manhaus' sponginess, trying to get at the heart beneath, though I doubt there's one to find. In the end, I don't even wrinkle his clothes. They are fused to and made out of the same materials as his puppet body.

I collapse by Manhaus' feet. He looks almost human again.

"There," he says, "feel better now? Rage all spent?"

I can only huff and puff. When I can finally speak all I say is: "I hate you. I hate you. I hate you. I hate you."

Manhaus grins. "Want to hate me even more?"

I repeat the litany.

"See this cigarette I'm smoking?"

"I see your fucking cigarette."

"It's a human by-product, too." He takes a final puff and grinds the cigarette (*humanarette?*) into the floor with his foot.

CHAPTER SEVEN

My new job isn't as labor intensive as the first, and I get to wear overalls rather than a loincloth. Still, it's so repetitive and mindless that I wish I could once again lug and connect bricks, ignorant of their composition.

What I do is pull the lever that opens the mouth of the kiln for all but four hours of the day. At least I hadn't been assigned corpse-loading detail. I see workers doing just that, and their lips are thin and pale and their eyes look like stones. I don't have to see the corpses, provided I keep my eyes focused on the lever and don't turn towards the conveyance system churning away behind me.

Nights are more difficult than those spent out in the field. The threat of rape is nonexistent, and everyone sleeps in tiny cots in a single large room, but I'll happily trade the sound of skeletal fingers tapping on walls and skinless feet sliding across floors for a million anal intrusions and biting bugs. I haven't seen anything yet—apart from a white thing that glided quickly across the hallway as I looked on from my cot a few nights back—but I feel a million swirling presences each time the lights go out. My work, I fear, has brought with it a curse, and the souls of all those whose bricks I've touched, even the ones I touched before changing jobs, glare at me with hatred. Now that the curtain's been lifted, I can't help but be aware of them.

I notice other workers, eyes wide and unsleeping on their cots night after night, and figure they're thinking similar thoughts.

Later, I ask the foreman if he can switch me to the nightshift, but it's out of the question.

At some point—there are no clocks and no windows, so time is meaningless apart from the workday itself—the foreman calls me into his office.

"You've worked hard in the years you've been here," he says.

"Years?"

He nods. "And, beginning tomorrow, you have three weeks to go wherever you please, provided you interact with no one and enter no buildings, though you may sleep here if necessary."

I'd long given up hope of ever leaving the factory. "Are you sure?"

"I wouldn't have brought you here if I weren't."

"Will I—uh—be able to do this again?"

"When you earn it."

"And when will that be?"

The foreman shrugs.

Late that same night, I'm awoken from a thin and fitful sleep by the sensation of something sliding over my wrist. Above me, the foreman looms.

"Some workers feel threatened and fight, so putting things on them while they sleep makes my job easier." He pauses to survey me. "You seem more like a pussy than a fighter, though."

Insults are customary, so his taunt doesn't faze me. I lift

96

my arm to see what the thing is, but the room is dark and my eyes bleary. Whatever it is, it looks almost like a black Casio wristwatch. "What is this," I ask.

"Just something to remind you when your time is up. It'll beep exactly three weeks from now. When it does, you must have it removed at the factory within three hours. If not, it—and you—will explode. Also, don't remove it early. It'll explode if you try that, too." The foreman's eyes roll back into this head, and I wonder if he's imagining my body bursting into wet and glistening hunks of meat. "At any rate, you are free to leave as soon as the morning shift starts."

I look at the watch. It seems innocent enough, but I trust the foreman knows what he's talking about. Once he leaves, I try to rest for the thirty or so minutes before the morning bell rings, but I just stare at the ceiling, not knowing what to do with myself and wondering if I'll be able to process even temporary freedom.

In the office, the foreman makes me strip out of my work uniform. I expect to be raped, but he just wants to give me a new set of clothes.

He places the collection on his desk. "You get to wear these clothes on your vacation."

"Where did they come from?"

"Oh, off a body. It seemed to be your size."

I look down at them. The pants—beige trousers—are very similar to what I wore on Earth. The T-Shirt says PARTY HARDY and features a dog on a surfboard against a festive Hawaiian backdrop. I hardly wore T-shirts, and never any that featured artwork or slogans. I don't like the underwear, either: red briefs.

He removes a final item from a bag on his desk. "And

these are your shoes."

"Stiletto heels!"

"Is there a problem?"

The last thing I want to do is jeopardize my vacation. "Uh —no. Not at all."

"Good, then get dressed."

I put the briefs on and grimace, as they're a size too small. The pants come next. I don't want the foreman ogling my package for any longer than necessary. Then I pull the shirt over my head, and finally, don the high-heels.

Once I'm fully clothed, the foreman holds the door open for me.

"Enjoy your vacation, you son of a bitch," he says.

It takes a while to get to the factory door with my new high heels, but, when I reach it, I feel like an elephant whose leg has been tethered to a pole. I stand by the door, unable to convince myself to move. What if I'm torn apart by house wolves, or stabbed, or shot, or eaten? After drawing a deep breath, I twist the knob and step unmolested into daylight. The sun appears foreign to me. I'd forgotten what it looked like—a giant red house-shaped body, beaming in the sky.

No taxi awaits me, so I assume I'll be walking to wherever it is I'm going.

The high-heels aren't at all pleasant. I don't think I'll ever get used to them, so I take the shoes off and cradle them in my arms. Though I'd rather toss them, I'll surely be called to task if they're missing at vacation's end.

I'm glad it's early. Most houses still sleep, and I feel like I have their world to myself. I enjoy this feeling, though I understand it's illusory.

Past the factory gates, I find myself in a residential neigh-borhood identical to the one I'd helped build. Further on, how-ever, the houses begin to lose their sameness, becoming sprawl-ing, sculpted, and, at times, *decadent*. Lawns are spacious and well manicured. Most feature in-ground pools with walls of trans-lucent green and identically colored gazebos. Lesser lawns are lucky to have empty planters perched atop featureless, sandy ground.

These places must be for those for whom austere cubes won't suffice. I try to imagine the types of houses who might live here—lawyers, doctors, engineers, or judges? Perhaps a leader of the House Mafia, provided such an organization exists.

Of course, there's also a slum. Grungy, decaying, and separated from the ritzy neighborhood by an expansive yet bar-ren field and a towering barbed wire fence that runs down its middle. These tenements are shaped like long sticks of butter—there must be hundreds of house families in each stick—and con-structed of the same green bricks, but even they seem less glow-ing and translucent, like degradation and depression have leached into them so deeply that even the processed dead feel malaise.

In time, I find myself back in the downtown area, near the spot where Manhaus had cut short my run a lifetime or two ago. So much has changed since then. The green spiral has indeed grown into a skyscraper. So immense, I doubt humans could have con-structed anything like it in my lifetime. Perhaps other places have become important libraries or fine schools or museums—they look suitably ornate—but I can't decipher the strange, swirly writing on their facades. Nor can I decipher similar writing on the host of giant billboards plastered against buildings up and down the street. Judging from the pictures, they showcase a wide variety of (often strange) consumable products and (inscrutable) house-based entertainment.

Golf cart-looking things like the one in which Manhaus had rode zoom by. The collective sound they make is similar to that of a thousand buzzing bees. Sculptures of great buildings tower over the street from green parks within circular intersections. I see the Parthenon, the Empire State Building, the Sears Tower, Biltmore Estates, the Tower of London, the Palace of Versailles, and others edifices whose foreign and sometimes ancient-looking architecture is unrecognizable.

The cityscape is stunning, but I still hate it. I want to tear the whole place down with my hands, brick by brick, and then defecate on it. It doesn't matter how many house souls I harm in the process. Even those who hadn't directly harassed me are guilty, even those who hold no grudge against humanity or even sympathize in private with our plight. *Fuck them.* Let everything in their lives burn.

"Human! Human! Human! Human," taunts a young house puppet, a boy-thing of about six or eight years.

It's as though that word alone is an insult, and perhaps it is.

I smile at him, though I display too many teeth.

The housemother notices my attention, grabs the child's arm, and hurries past.

Night falls. I try to sleep on the bench, but a cop walks over and prods me with his Billy club until I have flashbacks. I try another bench and, less than an hour later, get poked again. Then I try an alley, and it's packed with homeless houses, clothed in tattered rags and stinking of strange fluids.

They've built a small campfire. It looks very warm—though the flame glows blue—but I can't find the courage to join their circle, staying, instead, on the periphery where I barely feel the fire's warmth.

They don't talk to me, but I see something in their eyes, a sort of distant kinship, and realize that, though they won't befriend me, they will do me no harm.

I reclaim my spot by the Sears Tower statue, and that's when I see her, sitting on a bench across the street from me, staring.

She has densely coiled blonde hair that appears as though someone has dumped mounds of thick golden spaghetti on her head. Her cheeks are rouged with dark red circles that stretch from the bottom of her window-eyes to the top of her door-lips. Her lashes are disproportionately long, and she wears a loud, floral print sundress that's not only evocative of the sixties, but looks as if it had been constructed out of a tablecloth.

Maybe she's not staring at all, and I'm just being paranoid. It's often hard to tell with puppet eyes. Still, hers look more real somehow. I don't know how to describe it, and I'm not sure what to think, but she's definitely looking at me and not the statue. Maybe she finds it odd that a male human sits with a pair of stiletto heels on his lap.

I stare back at her with as much intensity as I can muster; she gets up and continues down the street.

I think nothing more of her.

But she's back a few hours later.

Perhaps a job takes her past the area where I sit, but that

doesn't explain her interest in me. I wish she'd look at the statue instead. It's more interesting than I am.

Now, she appears to read a magazine. I know it's a ruse. She glances up from the pages whenever she thinks I'm not looking, but I'm always looking.

Does she wish me ill? Is she mentally unbalanced? Is she planning to attack?

Maybe she'll go away if I ignore her.

No, she won't.

That night, in the alley with the bums, I dream of her.

First: a close-up of her face. My vision pulls back, and I see her in the factory, working—*really* working—the lever that opens the kiln. In fact, she's giving it a hand job, and the lever grows longer and fatter with each stroke.

My vision shifts again, to the corpse-laden conveyer belt. I've been lashed to it, and my body buckles in a futile attempt to escape. I didn't see her do it, but I know it's the house-woman who's trapped me here.

When the mouth of the kiln opens, the dream perspective shifts to my own. The fire inside draws closer until all I see is a blue blaze that first tastes, then envelops, and then changes me.

When my brick exits the kiln, the woman picks it up, but doesn't put it with all the others. She dumps it in a bin marked DEFECTIVE and leaves the factory through the front door.

CHAPTER EIGHT

The next morning, I awake to find a sheet of paper taped to the wall above me. There's writing on it, and I'm surprised to see it's in English:

I'm sitting on your bench. When I see you, I'll start walking. Follow me, but leave at least 20 paces between us. Don't try to interact with me and don't cause a scene.

I peek my head out from the alley and see the woman on the bench by the Sears Tower statue, waiting. I duck my head back inside.

Could this be a test? The supervisor told me to have no interaction with houses, but I feel too wrapped up in mystery to back down. If it's a test, then I'll just have to fail.

I try not to think of potential repercussions or of the dream as I exit the alley. The woman spots me. She nods discretely, after which she gets up and walks away at a leisurely pace. I follow, but feel like something's missing. It's the stilettos. I've left them back in the alley.

Fuck 'em.

Appearing inconspicuous is hard, being that I'm the only human on the street. I catch a number of sideways glances, most of them furtive, but the majority rushes past, too involved in their own lives to acknowledge mine.

A theater lets out. The chatter outside the lobby is maddening. *Meh-me-muh-meh-me-muh*—that's what it sounds like when dozens of houses rattle off in a confined space. I cover my ears until I'm a block away.

I return my attention to the woman, and just in time, too. She removes a battered tin can from her purse and places it discretely on a windowsill once there are no pedestrians between us. I pick it up. Inside, another note:

I'm stopping at my apartment. Take this can and pretend to be a beggar outside my door. I'll leave it unlocked, but don't enter if anyone's watching.

We walk for five more blocks until she places her palm against a pad outside a loft-style apartment above a clothing store. I stop walking and begin rattling my can.

Most just ignore me, or sneer as they pass. Perhaps I should say something:

"Money please."

"You'd just spend it on *targulu*," a house hisses.

I have no idea what *targulu* is, but feel like the lowest-of-the-low just the same.

A group of street punks pass and make eyes at me. I want to flee to the relative safety of the house-woman's apartment. Still too many people, though. Must play it cool.

An hour seems to pass, and I have just one measly coin in my cup —as green and translucent as the bricks, featuring the bust of Manhaus on the obverse and a coat of arms on the reverse—but at least crowds are thinner now.

I look left. Then right. Someone's a block down, but he's engrossed in the House Heaven equivalent of a cell phone. A clump of pedestrians chat amongst themselves a block up, but they don't face me.

Time to move. I slip through the door and find myself at the bottom of a narrow staircase hemmed in by walls. It's the perfect place to get trapped, or jumped, or killed.

The stairs buzz beneath my toes. How many more ghosts are inside me now, I wonder.

The door at the top of the flight is ajar. I pause before opening it. When I do, the woman seizes my wrist. From her dress pocket, she withdraws a knife, long and sharp. She's a psychopath, and she's going to send it right through my heart.

Instead, she starts sawing at the bomb around my wrist.

"Don't do that," I scream. "I'll explode!"

"It's just a ruse. I work for Manhaus. I should know."

She hacks for a few more seconds. The watch breaks free, and I don't explode.

"Told you it was a ruse, though it will blow up when your three weeks are over." She walks to the couch and pats a house-print cushion. "Take a seat. Relax."

I obey, but do so warily. "Who are you?"

"Don't you know?"

"No, I don't."

"I'm Helen."

"What? You mean *my* Helen?"

"Yours and yours alone."

This has to be some sort of trick. I look the woman over, my gaze unforgiving. Her structure, translated in puppet form, is reminiscent of Helen's, but, being a single-story, box-like structure, Helen wasn't of uncommon design (though she was of uncommon character).

"If you're Helen, then tell me something only she would know."

She unfastens three buttons on her dress, spreads the fabric

105

apart, and I see the two scars that the kitchen knife had left in her abdomen long ago.

"Oh my god," I rasp, and nothing else matters. I wrap my body around her, hugging her tightly so she might never leave me again. Her fabric emanates no warmth, but that doesn't matter, either. Her presence is all I need, and I don't even care she exists in hideous puppet form.

My brain replays something she'd just said: *I work for Manhaus, so I should know.*

I pull away from her. "Did you say you work for Manhaus?"

"Yes, but—"

I run my fingers through my hair. I feel like flailing, then like jumping out the window. "I can't believe you're working for that son of a bitch! You know what the green bricks are made of? You know what he does?"

She nods.

"And yet you do his bidding?"

She says nothing, just nods again. I want her to say something, *anything*. She needs to explain herself, and I have no intention of letting this pass. Invectives fly.

"He killed R'yony, the only human friend I've ever had! Turned him into a fucking brick as I watched! Maybe I was right when I called you a bitch!"

She bristles at the sound of the word, but composes herself quickly. "You want to know why I took this job?"

"Yeah, I do."

"Do you *really* want to know?"

"Spill it."

"My job is to track those on vacation by creating and maintaining a computerized database for the government. You'd—"

"I'm not impressed by what you do for Manhaus and his

cronies!"

"Let me finish," she hisses.

I cringe and say nothing further.

She composes herself. "The odds were in your favor that you'd appear in the system—you weren't young or lame enough to be turned into a brick—so I applied for my position and was accepted. Though I hated what I was about to do—and still hate it now—I was happy because I had hope that, one day, I'd find you."

"You did all this for me?"

"Also moved when your info came up on the *pending* screen, left my home in the suburbs, tossed everything to come here. That was over a month ago, but I knew you'd make your way downtown eventually, and I promised myself I'd walk the streets until I found you."

"I—oh my god—I'm *touched.*"

But Helen doesn't look touched; she looks *pissed.* There's palatable anger in her eyes, and I'd never seen anything more than plastic and paint in puppet eyes before.

"Yet you call me a *bitch*! Were my sacrifices not enough for you?"

"I had no idea. I jumped to conclusions. I—"

"Maybe you want me to do more. Should bleed for you, too?" She takes the knife and holds it over her left wrist. "Should I begin sawing now?"

"No, please no!"

She throws the blade to the floor, and I cringe as it clatters. "I never intended to waste blood on you, anyway!"

I feel like a fleck of mud, or, better yet, fly shit. "I hate myself," I blubber. "I didn't want this—I—Oh god, I suck. I—"

She leans in closer. "Excuse me?"

Try as I might, I can say no more.

Helen looks at me for a few seconds, like she expects me to say something coherent. When I don't, she stalks off in a huff, past the living room into the hallway. I hear her slam a door. Then I hear it lock.

And I walk to the window and stare at the featureless wall on the other side, motionless, my hand against the sill, until the last light goes out in the sun.

Finally, I return to the couch. I stand above it for a while, not sure if I'm worthy to place my filthy man-body atop her belongings. Tiredness gets the best of me, though, and I lay down. A part of me wants to get up, run to the door she hides behind, throw it open, and, with fists raised, beg humbly for forgiveness, but I'm sure she'll throw something hard at my head, if not take if off entirely.

Perhaps I deserve to have my head taken off. The room seems blacker than it should, and the ghosts are back. I close my eyes and close my ears. It makes little difference. They're inside me, and Helen's the only thing that can exorcise them. Due to my stupid, stupid mouth, they're going to be with me for all time, and Helen will haunt me, too.

I'm still awake when she leaves the bedroom at dawn. The last ghost had swirled away just minutes earlier.

"Carlos," she says.

I can't turn to her, not yet.

"Are you awake?"

I peek my head above the cushions. Helen's dressed in the same clothes as last night, and they look slept in. She has bags under her eyes; her shoulders slump.

"I'm awake," I manage.

She walks over the couch. I sit up so she can sit down.

"I'm sorry for last night. I only exploded because I hate what I do." She places her hand on my knee. "You were right to say what you said. I admit that now, and hope you'll accept my apology."

"I do. But are you going to quit your job, now that you've found me?"

Her tone is flat, perfunctory. "No."

"But why not?"

"Because Manhaus doesn't allow anyone to quit without *very* good reason."

An epiphany: "House Heaven sucks for houses too, doesn't it?"

"Only because of Manhaus and those like him," Helen replies.

"You work for the guy, so you must know things about him the average house doesn't."

"But I've only seen him once, and that was at orientation for work. Manhaus stays behind the scenes."

"He doesn't stop by your workplace to check up on you?"

"No, and thank *Goharmarmah* he doesn't, because I work at home."

"*Goharmarmah*?"

"That's what houses call God."

"I see, but what's special about Manhaus anyway? And why is he the only house who's not always a puppet?"

"Some say he's the product of the union of man and house before houses got glorified bodies."

"How's that possible?"

"Somehow, and this is unthinkable, his pre-existent *akuranamahana* was so strong that it fertilized the human seed spilled within a house mother. Thus, he was born as neither man nor house, but an amalgamation of the two."

"Akuramanahabalab?"

"No, *Akuranamahana.*"

"I meant *what does it mean.*"

"It's the primal core of the house soul."

I wonder if Helen's Akababalabalab—or whatever it's called—had been strong enough to conceive a child on Earth. Maybe it had been, and I was too blind and stupid to take advantage of her fertility. But what if our child grew up to be another Manhaus?

"I guess it's only natural that such an entity would make a power play or two," Helen continues, and I feel guilty for not having paid attention to the last few things she'd said. "But things weren't supposed to be this way. Prophecy had promised us otherwise."

Covering my tracks: "Is there a book of prophecy?"

She nods.

"Do you have a copy?"

Pointing to a bookcase on the other side of the room: "It's right over there."

I arise, but Helen tells me to stay put. She walks to the case and brings a lumpy, fleshy, and perhaps sentient grimoire back to the couch.

"Should I touch it?"

"Of course, it won't bite."

I reach out and, with wary hands, stroke the cover. Somewhat moist, it pulses beneath my fingers, and I wonder if there are veins and blood beneath what I can only consider *skin.*

"Are all house books like this?"

"No, it's only this way because it's from the Mother. This is *The First Book of House Heaven*, and every house has a copy."

"I see—uh—would you mind holding it while we look?"

"Not at all. I imagine you might find it repulsive." She tries to open the book, but it fights her for a few moments, the front cover whipping back and forth like the wing of an angry bat. After a few knocks against its spine, the thing behaves and lies flat.

Inside, it looks like any other tome, though the pages are somewhat thicker than normal and have a faint scarlet tinge. The first thing I see is a drawing of a man/house hybrid that's similar-to-but-not Manhaus. He wears tight, almost spandex-looking trousers and a frilly frock. A white powdered wig conceals his hair.

A caption beneath the picture: *Houseingham Walshgeorg.*

"Why is it in English?"

"It's not," Helen explains. "You only see it that way because it's your language. Anyway, Houseingham Walshgeorg is our Founding Father, the first house to break away from structure and discover his inner being. It's said that through him alone are we able to abandon Earthly form and become spiritual bodies."

"So, he's kinda like your messiah?"

"He was supposed to return to usher in a thousand years of peace and prosperity immediately following our entry into House Heaven. We got Manhaus instead."

"I hate to break it to you, but it sounds like Houseingham Walshgeorg isn't real."

She looks very wistful now. "I outgrew believing in him long ago, but a lot of other houses haven't. They still think he's coming back, even after the prophecy failed." She forces the book closed. "But let's go have breakfast. There's no reason to think of such things."

"I thought houses didn't eat."

"It's not necessary, but I like doing things that were impossible back when I was wood and brick and siding. It's hard spending thousands of years unable to do even the basic things that those who live inside you do."

I'm confused. "Thousands of years? But you weren't even around a hundred years ago."

"Not in the form you knew, but I was around just the same."

"Reincarnation?"

Helen nods.

"Do you remember anything about your past lives?"

"Most are fuzzy, if that. But I barely remember being by a river, and there was a young girl who lived in me, and I liked her very much, but she died young."

"I'm sorry."

"Well, that was a long time ago. I also remember being in a big city—this might have been right before I became your house because there were cars near the end, but they looked very different from the ones you know. People had big, lavish parties in me. Then I went away."

"Do you know how you died?"

"Can't say for sure, but I think it was to make room for a skyscraper. Times were changing."

"Is that all you remember?"

"I might have been a pyramid at one point, but I don't think I was Egyptian. I think I was something much older."

"Fascinating," I say, and mean it.

"But I'm really hungry, and if you want to talk more about this, we'll have to do so in the kitchen."

Her kitchen is nice and neat, if a little cramped. Oddly enough, it's an almost exact replica of the kitchen inside Helen when she was my house.

"Did you do this intentionally," I ask.

"If you mean the décor, then yes. In my old place, all rooms were identical to the ones inside me on Earth. I've only had time to replicate two of them here, though I hope to get the living room next month."

"I could help, if you want. I know *everything* about your old interior."

"Thanks, I may take you up on that." She walks over to a counter and removes a mixing bowl. "I'm in the mood for toast and gravy. Want some?"

"Sure. That would be great."

She whips up some green batter, and I wonder why she's whipping any manner of batter for gravy. I question her.

"Oh, now you're being silly. This isn't the gravy. This is the toast."

"Do you have to cook it?"

She looks confused. "Cook toast?" Then she pours the batter into a mold and begins sprinkling powers on it from a collection of jars lining the counter.

I'm not sure I want the toast and gravy anymore.

A few minutes later, she lays a plate before me. What it contains reminds me of Helen when she was a horrible, molten corpse. It makes a *blurbling* sound and emits plosive puffs of steam from craters like tiny lava vents.

I pick up the fork. It feels heavy in my hands.

"Nope, I'm not done yet. Still have to add the gravy."

She leans a decanter over my plate. The gravy exits a spout with the appearance and consistency of a semi-liquefied cow patty, but, at the very least, it causes the vents to stop steaming.

The fork feels even heavier now, and I want to hurl. "Ummmmm," I say. "Looks delicious!"

"You're lying."

"I'm sorry, but it really is gross. You're not mad, are you?"

"Not mad, just amused. You never know how something tastes until you try it."

"True," I smile, but it comes out a frown. Then I stick the fork into the toast and gravy. It quivers as I stab it, almost as though it's a living thing, and my actions bring it pain.

Helen senses my unease. "It only looks like it's hurting."

I lift the still-quivering bite and, with eyes closed, bring it to my mouth, though I stop before it reaches my tongue.

"This isn't at all like the toast and gravy I'm used to. Are you sure it won't kill me?"

She sits her own plate down and takes a seat. "Well, I've never seen a human eat house food before..."

I decide to bite the bullet and begin chewing. The flavor is surprisingly pleasant, though it tastes nothing like toast and gravy.

"You're supposed to chew with your mouth open," she admonishes sternly.

Shocked, I drop my fork. "I'm sorry. I really don't know anything about House etiquette."

"It's just that my mother made such a big deal about it..."

I make sure my lips are parted as I chew. "Am I doing it right?"

"No, wider."

A glob of toast and gravy falls from my mouth into my lap. "Better?"

"*Perfect.*"

"And how about my elbows? Am I supposed to put them on the table?" I demonstrate.

"Yes, but not in *that* position. This is how you do it." She contorts her elbows into a number of strange shapes and permutations that my bones will never reproduce.

"Would you be too offended if I didn't do it that way?"

"I'm not *that* anal about table etiquette."

"Good, because I'd hate to offend you again. I don't know if I've expressed it yet, but I'm so glad to see you, even in puppet form." I realize I may have just made a faux pas, a *really bad* one. "Oh god, I'm sorry! I just—uh—never imagined your true form would be *this*."

"It's not my true form."

"Then change back. Let me see you as you are."

"You see houses as puppets because it's your greatest fear, and I can't change that." She scoots her chair closer to mine. "But now that you know my appearance isn't real, can you look past it?"

I don't want to be shallow—it would be like me divorcing a human Helen after an accident had disfigured her—but I want her old form back, only vocal and warm. I don't love the Sid and Marty Krofft nightmare she's become, but still love the soul within the shell, and hope the physicality I see never causes me to forget this.

"I know I can," I tell her, and hate myself for it.

After breakfast, we return to the living room where she shows me some personal stuff. We start with a few trinkets and baubles that are special to her, mostly for sentimental reasons—things given to her by family and friends—and conclude with a photo album, which I find most interesting.

She leafs through the album. "This is my great grandmother, Helnashaka Blomonstrovitch Blaknavarka, but I just called her

Helna. I remember her as being a tiny lady with spindly legs and a bowed back."

"How old was she when she died?"

Helen looks confused. "She isn't dead."

"But you're talking about her in past tense."

She doesn't acknowledge me. Instead, she turns the page to an 8x10 portrait of a matronly house that resembles an older, overweight Helen. "This is my mother. I called her M'lana, but that's what all house children call their mothers."

"Are you the only house in your family with a normal first name?"

"My real first name isn't Helen, it's Halanatavakia."

"Oh. What's your full name?"

"Halanatavakia Sloptavski Blaknavarka."

"Can I still call you Helen?"

"Of course. It's sweet."

"Well, Halanatavakia is a pretty name, too." I hate lying, especially to Helen, so I deflect guilt by changing the subject. "So, how about your father? Do you have pictures of him?"

"We don't have fathers. Male houses just are."

"I see. Can I hold the album?"

"Sure."

I take it from her and flip through the pages. The pictures all seem to be of houses considerably older than Helen. "Are any of these still living? If so, they must be ancient now."

"Well, I'm as old as my mother, and grandmother, and great-grandmother, and all other house souls in House Heaven. I don't think we can die—at least I've never heard of it happening —though some of us are taken to retirement homes."

"But if you're all the same age, shouldn't you all be in a home?"

"I don't know how houses are selected. It's just another

one of Manhaus' rules; if you get the letter, you go to a home."
Helen's bottom lip twitches. "My mother was taken late last year."

"Do you visit her?"

She shakes her head, which makes her full body turn,
since she has no neck. "No, no one visits the homes."

"So how do you know you're not being lied to?"

"I *don't*. I just have to believe my relatives are in good
hands and leave it at that."

Perhaps I shouldn't press the matter. "I understand," I
say, then close the photo album and sit with her, silently on the
couch.

Soon, Helen has to go to work. I ask if I can accompany her. She
says yes.

I watch from the floor as she types on a computer that sits
on a desk in an otherwise empty room. The computer, I assume,
came from the belly of the Mother, as its monitor is a reptile/
demon head with an open maw. The database that Helen maintains is visible inside the thing's mouth, hemmed in by rows of
pointy razor-teeth. An umbilical cord of sorts connects the monitor to the computer itself, which looks to be a too-large tongue,
or, worse yet, a flaccid monster penis. The keyboard, however,
looks like a keyboard, and it's connected to the tongue-penis
thing by a standard cord.

"Can you check e-mail on that?"

"You mean *häuser-mail*?"

"I guess I do."

"Yeah, I can check it. Can do on-line banking, too, but
that's about all on this heap of junk." The display inside the mouth
flickers, and she knocks the monitor with her knuckles, causing
the thing to unleash a wounded howl. The screen quickly returns

to normal, and Helen resumes typing.

After work, she relaxes in front of the television. The TV isn't unusual per se, but, with its thick wood paneling and rounded, black and white picture tube, it would look more at home in 50s suburbia than House Heaven. She flicks through the channels with a large, clumsy-looking remote before choosing a live telecast of a sporting event.

It's the most confusing game I've ever seen. The goals— four of them—are in the center of the field, in the form of long poles atop which tiny nets are strung. The point doesn't seem to be getting the ball into these nets, which seem more decorative than anything. Three teams hold various sized boxes in outstretched hands. Once a whistle sounds, they run around with these boxes, sometimes throwing them at an opposing team's players, who feign death on the field if and when hit. The referee also has a box, a large one that completely covers his head.

Helen claps and pumps her fist when one of the teams does something. "Yes! I went to South Housnia University, you know. Good ole SHU!"

My blank expression seems to concern her, but I never liked sports, even the kind I could understand.

"You're not for Housevania U are you?"

"I've never heard of any of those places, so I really don't have the nostalgia you have. Sorry."

She looks disappointed. "Well, let's turn it. The game is getting me too worked up, anyway. I want something that'll make me sleepy." She scans the channels, looking for more sedating fare, until she comes upon a debate show on a political network.

"Want to watch this? You might find it educational."

"I really can't understand a word of it."

"I'll translate. Maybe you can pick up a little house along the way."

I nod—though I expect to be bored silly—and turn to the TV. Thanks to Helen, I know the debate flickering on the screen goes something like this:

HOUSE #1 (*has a little Hitler moustache*): All humans should die!

HOUSE #2 (*swirls a glass of wine*): No, humans should be kept alive and working. Otherwise, it's you (*he points to HOUSE #1*) and you (*he points to the audience*) and you (*then he points to the camera*) who'll have to shoulder the burden of building our cities. Did any of you expect to come here for *that*?

HOUSE #3 (*is pencil-thin and looks Jewish for a house*): The humans who are here should be given amnesty from undue persecution, and the better workers should be paid and allowed to mingle in House society. Anything less is barbarism. I ask you, are we no better than the worst human imaginable?

A HECKLER IN THE AUDIENCE: No amnesty for the humans! Work 'em overtime!

THE HOUSE BEHIND HIM: The humans here have done much to build our city. We owe it to them to acknowledge that, at the very least.

ANOTHER HOUSE: Much? Hell, they've done everything!

A FEMALE HOUSE IN THE AUDIENCE (*looks at both with scorn*): Man lovers!

THE DISTINGUISHED MODERATOR (*motioning to black suited, gun-toting guards in the background*): Now, now. We'll have audience Q&A after the debate is over.

(*The two houses are escorted away, violently. The female house smirks at them just before they disappear behind the stage; the heckler flips them a bird.)*

HOUSE #3: As I was saying, we should give to those deserving. If they weren't all so downtrodden and poor, then humans wouldn't be a threat to our society, though I feel this threat is more perceived than actual.

HOUSE #1: They're poor because they deserve to be poor! It's their lot in life!

HOUSE #3: You, sir, are a bigot!

HOUSE #1 *rises up from the shared table and, with oversized foamy hands, begins throttling* HOUSE #3. THE DISTINGUISHED MODERATOR *doesn't seem to mind.* HOUSE #2 *looks somewhat concerned, but not concerned enough to help.*

It continues for a few minutes until Helen shuts off the TV. "That didn't make me tired either, but to hell with it. Time for bed."

I make my way from the armchair to the couch.

"What are you doing?"

"Uh, getting ready to sleep."

"Not there."

"Then where?"

Her tone is different now, lilting. "I want you to sleep in my bed tonight."

My pulse quickens, but not necessarily in a good way. "With you?"

"Of course."

"Are you sure that would be—"

"Yes, it would be very appropriate. Besides, you look so lonely on the couch."

She opens the door to her bedroom. Like the kitchen, it's similar to the corresponding room that had been inside her on Earth, only feminized. I sure didn't have lace doilies on the dresser, decorative perfume bottles on a bookshelf, and pictures of house-shaped flowers (or any flowers for that matter) on my walls. The only real break from the ordinary is the bed. At least I think it's a bed. The sheets and covers on it look ordinary, but the thing itself is a huge, irregularly shaped slab of pulsing muscle that breathes almost indiscernibly.

"Will it eat me?"

She laughs. "No, silly. It's just a bed."

"You sure about that?"

"It came straight from the Mother. I haven't had the time to get a new one, and I kind of like its squishy feel."

She strips down to her bra and panties and, without hesitation, ensconces herself in the muscular folds of her strange bed. It makes sloshing sounds when she lies on it, but doesn't breathe any heavier than before, nor does it move in any questionable or threatening way.

She doesn't appear to be in danger, so I make my way to the bed and lift the covers. Before I can get in Helen says, "Take off your pants."

"What?"

"You didn't sleep in your pants when you lived in me, did you."

"But I'm not wearing boxers. I'm—"

"Go on, you can be comfortable around me."

I draw a few deep breaths and unbutton my pants, holding them up by my waist for a few seconds before letting them drop to the floor. I keep my shirt on.

She looks at my briefs. "Ummmm, red."

Embarrassed, I cover myself with both hands and say

nothing.

"Now you're just being silly." She pats the covers. "Come to bed."

I get in and pull the sheets up to my neck quickly so she doesn't see my body and my semi-concealed man-part for too long.

She cuts off the bedside lamp, but there's still enough light coming from the street outside for my eyes to make out shadows of furniture and her face through the gray. I look up at the ceiling for a while, feeling weird to be semi-naked with Helen, especially when she's semi-naked, too.

I don't know what to do. Maybe nothing and let Helen go off to sleep. Still, it doesn't make sense that she would bring me to her bed if she didn't want to talk. I look over at her. She faces me and her eyes are open.

Maybe she's waiting for me to start the conversation. But what should we discuss? Shows on TV? What we're going to have for breakfast tomorrow? The weather in House Heaven? No, it's time to delve into *important stuff*, even if it's the type of conversation I'd rather not have. I *must* talk about certain things and relieve myself of guilt. Otherwise, it'll fester forever. This is surely what she's waiting for – and perhaps even leading me into – though I may be wrong, and am not sure why I have to be in my underwear to unload.

"Do you remember when you were dead, and you had melted, and I was beside you," I ask.

Helen nods, and my stomach starts to churn and feel heavy.

"Well, I hate I said those things to you then." I pause. "You heard them, didn't you?"

"I did."

"How can you still love me? I don't know if *I* could love me after that."

"You were under stress, and mourning too. People who mourn sometimes get emotional and say things they don't mean."

"You weren't even a little mad?"

She waits a few seconds. "A little, perhaps. I'm only *housian,* and my emotions sometimes override my better judgment."

"Okay, you can forgive me for that, but how about when I stabbed you? Is that forgivable, too?"

"That happened before you really knew me. I'm not even certain you understood I was alive then, and I think that's why you did it, to make yourself guilty and convince yourself I was."

"Maybe you're right."

"Besides, I didn't feel it, and, by the time I became a house soul, the wound was nothing more than a scar." She pauses. "But I want to apologize, too."

I'm taken aback. "For what?"

"For crashing down on you. It was the last thing I wanted to do, but it was my body's time to die."

"And I'm sorry for not understanding and getting mad when it did."

"But let's not think of those times. Not when you're here and warm beside me."

I find her choice of words curious. "Would you still want me beside you if I had my old body?"

"Do I have to spell it out for you? I've wanted to lay into you even before I was glorified."

"*Lay into me?*"

She scoots in closer. "Yes."

"I – I – I'm a virgin."

Closer still: "Then I'll be gentle with you."

In truth, I don't want her to be gentle. I want her to tear into me, rip me apart, but, but—oh god, it would be like fucking the foreman, the construction site guard, the mad scientist, Manhaus, and all the things I've grown to hate. Is this *racism* festering inside me? I can't judge all houses by the acts of a few—even the acts of the majority—but it's easier to let the past dictate the present. "I—I don't think I'm ready," I finally stammer, "and I don't know if I'll ever be."

"How old are you?"

"29, I think. Well, I was 29 when I entered House Heaven."

She removes her panties beneath the covers and tosses them to the floor. "Believe me, you're ready." Then she unfastens her bra.

"Are you sure you should do that!"

Her house knockers are massive and well formed. "That and more," she says, climbing atop me. I feel very awkward now. Looking up, I imagine Manhaus' face superimposed over hers.

"I love your underwear," she continues, and begins massaging my nuts through them, and I almost-but-not-quite overshoot the waistband. "And I want you to keep them on when you do me."

Manhaus' face dissolves; Helen's returns. "But how will I—"

"Just pull them down around the base of your scrotum." She smiles. "In fact, let me do that for you."

Her fingers tickle my abdomen as she grasps the waistband and pulls. My cock and balls spill out. She's the first person—yes, I think of her as a person now—to see them since I showered in high school gym class, but that wasn't at all erotic, in fact it was the just opposite.

"I want it to be just like that movie I saw you watch."

"What? You mean *Roadhouse*?" Everything feels slightly off kilter again. "With Patrick Swayze?"

"Yeah, that's the one. I want you to be my regular Tuesday

night thing."

"I think it was Saturday."

"No matter. Just get inside me."

Still, I hesitate, biting my lip. I've long hungered for consummation, but, at the same time, I've long feared it, and never imagined doing her while she looked so *puppety*.

"Come on, fuck me."

I draw in a deep breath, but it's not enough, so I draw in two more. Then I penetrate her warm and well-insulated folds, my virginity a memory. My penis suddenly feels trapped between two very rough pieces of carpet. I don't like the sensation, at all, but that's before natural juices kick in and dampen her upholstery. It's more pleasurable now, less chafing, and I can finally get into the act.

I pump my hips with increasing speed and fluidity. It makes me feel like a machine, and I love it. I even start to enjoy the sensation of my underwear bunched up beneath my balls. Juices roll around inside them, churning. They will be released shortly.

Suddenly, light spills from her vagina, then from her mouth. It's almost enough to make me stop, but I'm too far in to pull out, and perhaps this is what's supposed to happen when people and houses have sex. I shield my eyes. Through my fingers, I watch her continued transformation. The puppet form disintegrates, becoming a bright and luminous body as her soul drops its mask.

"You have found my secret chamber," she whispers, her mouth full of stars.

I come with a shudder, and her body brightens, enveloping the entire room with light until I see nothing else. But I'm not content to merely view her soul. I link with it, become it, and all there is or ever shall be is *light*.

At the end of this seemingly eternal moment, the bedroom returns and her puppet form subsumes luminosity, but its reemergence doesn't bother me now that I know what rests beneath the illusion.

I pull my briefs the rest of the way up. Then I collapse on my side, panting heavily.

"Don't pull the covers up," she says. "I want to watch you as I fall asleep. I find the human body sexy in its impermanence."

And so I don't. I revel in her gaze, staring into her eyes until they close, and I close mine.

CHAPTER NINE

Early the next morning, I exit the bedroom. Helen is already in the living room, on the couch watching the news.

I'm still in my underwear, but not embarrassed in the least. I've also torn the sleeves off my t-shirt and turned it into a muscle shirt, and, true to its slogan, I'm finally ready to PARTY HARDY. I'd just stared at myself in the mirror for minutes, posing, flexing, and positioning my bulge for maximum visual impact. I look *perfect*.

She turns and sees me. I lift my arms above my head and undulate my hips rhythmically. Bringing my hands down slowly, I run them over both sides of my body, lingering at the naughty parts. In turn, she tears off her dress—ripping it in the process—and we do it on the couch.

An hour later, and she's at the fridge removing a pre-made sandwich from a cellophane-wrapped container. I take her from behind (*like a thief in the night*) and we do it on the floor, traveling from one end of the room to the other on our backs, and share the sandwich later.

After that, we have sex on top of the TV, and then against the living room wall, and then against the opposite living room wall, and then against the same wall as the first time we did it in the living room. Finally, we do it on the stove.

When I fall asleep, I fall asleep atop and inside her.

When we wake up—simultaneously—we do it again until we pass out, and then, when I wake up early in the morning—ready and raring to start—she's already fucking me.

I don't think Helen worked at all today, but oh well. Life is a whirlwind of sex, that and nothing more—sex in the morning, sex in the evening, sex at suppertime. Apart from one little sandwich, sex is all we eat. It's what we live and breathe, too. I think we even have sex while asleep, though I have no way of knowing this. I am, however, certain that three days have passed since I last wore pants.

"Do you think maybe we should just—I don't know—give it a rest?"

Helen is sprawled across the sofa, her body limp. "Maybe."

"Want to watch TV or something?"

"Yeah, that's a good idea." She reaches for the remote, but has trouble grasping it, and some time passes before she has the thing in her hand.

While more than happy to relax, I find myself thinking of sex each time a commercial interrupts the inane sitcom we watch. I sip on a glass of distilled wood spirits—a *housian* sedative—to mute those feelings as I sink deeper into the couch.

Helen sips a glass of distilled wood spirits, too. I nod at her, knowingly.

We spend the proceeding days getting our hormones evened out. It wasn't easy going at first, but excess has finally given way to a more balanced structure in our daily lives.

128

It feels good having finally reached baseline. I'm comfortable with Helen even when we're just sitting around the apartment, doing nothing special. Not even my forced shut-in status bothers me. My life back on Earth accustomed me to it, but now I'm shut-in *with* Helen rather than *in* her, and that makes everything I feel, see, hear, and taste good in our little, self-contained area of House Heaven—the garden where my happiness finally grows.

Helen and I are sitting together on the sofa—the TV's on, but we're not watching it—when someone knocks on the door.

My eyes widen. I freeze mid-kiss. Helen ends the make-out session, grabs my arm, and pulls me to the bedroom so roughly it hurts. "Get under the bed," she commands.

I look down. While, the top is muscle-smooth, the bottom is dank, snotty, and drippy.

"You might want to take off your clothes first," she says.

"Can't I go to the closet instead?"

"No, closets are social places."

"Really?"

"Yes, really! Now get undressed and *go!*"

I obey, tossing my clothes in a hamper so they won't be seen. Helen hurries to the door, but turns before she exits. "Promise me you won't come out, no matter what happens."

"But—"

"*Promise me!*"

I cringe. "I promise."

She shuts the door, and I slide beneath the bed. Suddenly, I feel like I'm in a monster's belly. I fear digestion. There's a clear plastic pan under the bed to collect the thick, mucus-like drippings so they don't ruin the floor. Perhaps Helen has neglected to drain it for a few days. It's full enough to slip and slide in.

The door in the living room opens, but I don't hear voices until they're in the hall. It sounds like there're three of them, including

Helen.

They enter the bedroom, and it's still hard to tell if they're agitated or talking normally. Isolating inflection in House language is impossible. Then I hear the closet door open and close. The voices are more muffled now. My relief is two-fold: I hate hearing Helen talk like a house, and things can't be too dire if they're happening in a social place (?) like the closet.

It sounds like they're all laughing, too. I wonder what they could be talking about: new dresses or hairdos, new jobs or new lovers (hopefully without mentioning me, and, if she does mention me, hopefully she'll tell them I'm a house). Whatever it is, I wish they'd hurry up, as I can't take being under this bed-thing much longer. The goop feels like it's slipping into my skin, rendering the epidermis soft and spongy. I hope it doesn't slough off. Though my glorified body could probably handle the loss, I'd hate having to go through life as a muscle-wrapped skeleton.

Hours seem to pass, but I can't say for sure. Beneath the bed, there is no time. I just keep sliding around in muck, hoping it doesn't collect too thickly around me and trap my body, if not fill my lungs.

Suddenly, someone—or something—crashes hard against one of the closet walls. Maybe someone just hit it with an elbow.

But the sound is repeated, and then repeated again. The houses in the closet start shouting. It reminds me of sounds assailants might make during beheading videos: "*Muhahajajahanaha mukhanayahu kaloopihardiharoo! Hagallalalah harn!*"

If I had pants, I'd piss them right now.

"*Ulharamaranka killhankra humalensah,*" the voices continue, two at once, and I might be wrong, but it sounds like they're saying "*kill humans*".

They shout another line, but I can't hear it as something—

perhaps a head—crashes five times in rapid succession against the wall. Somebody's getting pummeled in there. That much is certain. Maybe it's Helen who's doing the pummeling. While I hope that's the case, it's not a safe assumption to make.

I must come to her aid.

I claw my way through the muck to the edge of the bed, but stop before I reach it, my body sliding back to the other side. I'd promised I'd stay, and I'd sooner die than break a promise with Helen.

No matter what I hear, I cannot leave my hiding place.

But the voices in the closet sound louder, angrier, and the banging's more ferocious than before. Something breaks.

Fuck the promise.

I start clawing again, but the door opens, and the more sedate *muh-muh-muh* sounds return. I try to isolate Helen's voice, but can't. Then I try to slide closer to the edge of the bed, so I can see how many feet have left the closet. The muck won't let me. It's almost as though it knows what I want and makes itself slicker to defy me. The bedroom door shuts.

Minutes later, it re-opens. Footsteps return; one set this time. Foamy feet stop by the bed. I feel my heart in my throat until the body leans down and I see my lover's face. "It's safe to come out," she says.

I slide out from the bed, looking as though I've just been born, naked and covered in goop. "What the hell just happened," I ask, eyes darting. "Are you okay?"

"What do you mean?"

"What do you mean *what do I mean*? It sounded like you were getting raped in there—or *murdered*!"

"Oh no, that's just the way we houses conclude social engagements—with lots of beating and banging around the closet."

"So, it's normal?"

She nods her upper body.

"Thank god. You really had me scared. Who were those people—I mean houses—anyway?"

"Friends from college. I tried to get them in the closest in the other room, but they expected to be entertained here."

"Why?"

"Secondary closets are reserved for acquaintances. Putting them in one would have been perceived as insulting, especially since I haven't seen them in years." Helen wipes a gob of goop from my forehead. "But I'm sorry for keeping you under there for so long. I couldn't just throw them out. It would have seemed suspicious."

"That's okay. They're gone now, and everything's fine." I look down at my body. "But I need to get all this stuff off me somehow."

"Why don't you take a bath?" Helen offers.

It sounds like a very good idea.

I sink into the tub and realize it's the first time I've bathed since entering House Heaven. The water is warm, steamy, and *thick*. It's weirdly relaxing, but, at the same time, reminds me too much of semen. When I arise, it sticks to me like a gel, and I have to towel myself off for almost thirty minutes before all the water (or whatever it is) is off.

Helen and I return to the TV, but, after the events of the day coupled with the warm and clingy bath, I'm too tired to pay much attention to whatever's flickering on the screen. I lay down on the couch, intending to close my eyes for a minute or two.

When I open them, the room is dark. Helen isn't here,

nor is she in the kitchen or the bedroom. Instead, I find her in the workroom, hunched over the computer.

"Damn it," she shouts, bringing her hand down hard on the desk.

I walk over to her. "What's wrong?"

"Nothing major. I just have to attend a series of meetings, beginning tomorrow."

"I thought you did all your work from home."

"I do, but I have to go to these things when they happen. It's only about once or twice a year, but they annoy the hell out of me." She shuts off the e-mail (*häuser-mail?*) program. "Think you can entertain yourself for three or four days?"

"I'm sure I'll find something to do. I'll just think of you and watch TV, I guess."

Helen laughs. "Is that all?"

"Well…"

"You know you could do other stuff, too. I have this neat Virtual Reality helmet. It's in the closet if you ever want to experiment with it."

"If it's so neat, then why is it in the closet?"

"It's an old version, not top-of-the-line anymore."

"Is it dangerous? Will it melt my brain?"

"Don't imagine so."

"I might use it, then."

Her gaze is more intense now. "Are you *sure* you can handle being alone? You won't do anything stupid, will you?"

"Don't worry about me. I can take care of myself. It'll be low-key, but I'll make the best of it."

I turn to her just after we bed down. "I want to have sex before you go."

"Save it, and it'll be even better when I get back."

"Are you sure?"

She nods.

"Really sure?"

"Yes."

"Really, really sure?"

"I'm sure as sure gets."

"How about oral sex, then?"

"Men," she says and laughs.

"Okay, I'll wait." I make a sad-puppy face. "Won't be easy."

"Well, I'll be just as ready as you when I get back." She grins. "So prepare yourself as soon as that happens, okay?"

I return the grin, then roll over and try to make myself sleep. It doesn't work. I'm far too horny, so I must jack off to expend excess energy, but wait until I'm certain she's no longer awake. I don't want her to think I'm a typical man, totally controlled by my penis, though I may very well be.

I try to be careful. Nevertheless, my seed spills onto the bed. When I go to rub it away, I find that the bed has already eaten it. I hope—really, *really* hope—that it's not capable of reproducing.

I see her off just before dawn.

"Now remember, don't let anyone in who's not me and always look through the peep hole. I don't expect visitors, and no one knows you're here, but it's best to be safe."

"Okay, I'll do this stuff."

"And don't feel awkward. Do what you want here. My place is yours."

"I'll remember that."

"Good," she kisses me on the cheek with lips that don't move. "See you in a few days."

CHAPTER TEN

I don't know what to do with myself. In lieu of making real plans, I spend the entire first day masturbating with my muscle shirt on and my underwear pulled down around my scrotum, just like Helen likes it.

It's not the same, though. My hand is my hand and Helen is sweet, sweet Helen. But maybe Helen can be a couch, so I fuck the tight space between two cushions on the sofa. It's a little better than my hand, and even reminds me of what doing her was like before she temporarily lost her puppet form, but it's still not Helen.

Oh god, I can't stomach the idea of masturbating anymore! If I do it again, I fear I'll die as the last drop of concentrated *me* spurts from the tip of my penis.

My legs are wobbly when I get off the couch. I make them carry me to the coffee table where the remote sits.

I watch house sports exclusively, and, in time, the games start to almost-but-not-quite make sense, even if I can't understand a word the announcers and commentators say. I root for Housezania and boo Apartmanopolis each time the players take the field.

"Go Housezania! Go!"

During half-time, I feel weird going through her fridge—raiding it, as it were—but hunger soon gets me over that hang-up, and Helen would understand. She wouldn't want her lover starving to death in the apartment of plenty.

Back in the living room, I drink house beer and munch sawdust flavored sausages and popcorn-esque kernels shaped like little people heads. I hope these aren't human by-products, but Helen doesn't strike me as the kind of gal who would stock such things in her pantry.

On the third day, anxiousness sets in. I want her back, even if she has to drop everything and leave Manhaus and his cronies hanging in the boardroom. I don't care; I need her now.

I can't even masturbate. It feels so phony.

Anxiousness turns to desperation, and I remember her saying something about having a Virtual Reality helmet. Perhaps artificial reality will make real reality seem less dire. It's worth a shot, at any rate.

I look in a box on the floor of the closet. There, I find house porn featuring a bunch of oily male houses flaunting insanely large penises. Embarrassed, I close the lid and try to forget I'd seen that.

There's nothing resembling a helmet either on the floor or on the shelf. I might be looking in the wrong closet, so I go to the second bedroom. I hadn't been inside it before. There isn't even a bed, and I suspect Helen uses this room for storage.

I find what has to be the Virtual Reality helmet sitting atop a shelf in the closet. When I place it on my head, everything's dark. This is probably because I haven't turned the thing on yet.

With the device still on my head, I feel up and down its sides until I locate a switch.

I flip it. A menu appears before my eyes, yellow words superimposed over a green background: *The Grand Library, The Manhausian Church, The Fountains of Housezania, The Museum of Contemporary Art*. This, I realize, is a travel-based virtual tour. I'd hoped for something sexier, but don't know how to change the program.

The *Museum of Contemporary Art* option sounds like the best bet. Seconds later, I stand—or *seem* to stand—outside the same gargantuan, spiral-shaped building that's only a few blocks from Helen's apartment. My mental viewfinder shifts, and suddenly I'm inside a thin yet surpassingly tall room. Sculptures dot the floor; paintings are hung all up and down a staircase that traverses the entire length of the spiral.

The helmet has zoom-in and zoom-out features, so I use them to view the lower-level displays. In sculpture, the housian form is glorified. I, however, see it in puppet form, which lends an air of absurdity to the bevy of huge, muscular bodies, Grecian-style clothing, statuesque poses, and laurel wedged ears. Only one piece out of many seems to be of a human form, and it's twisted and deformed and bent, almost like a gargoyle.

I abandon the zoom features and, in a sense, walk up the steps. The paintings that line the walls are photo-realistic. Most sing the virtues of simplicity, honor, and obedience. Others feature the bust of some famous house-guy whose importance is unknown to me, unless, that is, the subject is Manhaus, who I often see wielding a sword or sitting astride a weird animal that must be House Heaven's answer to a horse.

I look for it, but there's no trace of the ultra-modern, the impressionistic, or the abstract here—no distorted forms, unnatural colors, or skewed focuses; nothing I couldn't see with my own eyes on any given day.

Higher still, I encounter the first in a series of banners, suspended from the ceiling at ever increasing altitudes. I wonder what they say. Something like

TRUE ART IS HOUSIAN ART

or

ART IS EMOTIONAL, NOT INTELLECTUAL

perhaps?

I remove the helmet before I reach the next banner, much less the top of the stairwell. I've seen enough.

Five days have elapsed. Perhaps I shouldn't worry, but I can't help it. I pace around the room, too agitated to watch TV or masturbate or use the helmet.

Can't she call? This place has to have a phone somewhere, or, at the very least, something that functions as the House Heaven equivalent. Even if I find one, I have no idea where to reach her, and, even if I locate a number, it might not be wise to call out. What if someone else answers? Houses don't address each other in English, and my doing so would surely arouse suspicion.

I can do nothing but wait.

And so I wait and wait. And wait and wait and wait and wait.

It's been over a week, and I'm no longer sure she's coming back.

139

Had she gotten lost somewhere? That makes no sense. Maybe there's been an accident.

Or maybe the problem is *me*.

Do I not satisfy her? Was she just humoring me in the past, and has she now grown sick of doing so? That would explain why she didn't want to have sex before leaving…

If I'd been able to say goodbye, then I might feel differently. I might be able to experience some closure. Now, I feel nothing but a sensation akin to standing by an open grave, and no manner of heating pad shall warm me tonight.

I dream for the first time since sleeping in that filthy back alley. Helen is again the subject.

She is naked and crawling all over a burly mustachioed house whose appearance reminds me of a construction site guard.

I become aware of myself, standing off in a dark corner, not wanting to watch—but watching just the same—as the guard thrusts his househood into her vagina. Helen rocks with his cock, her body rippling like a waveform and whipping like a lasso.

It's almost supernatural, the way she moves. She doesn't go *that* crazy when we make love, and I realize, with a cold, sinking feeling, that she never will.

Helen turns to me: "You could never be house enough for me," she says venomously, her tongue now bifurcated, and even her face has scales.

Then she returns to fucking, but I don't see much more of the act. My view suddenly shoots forward, across the room and to the window. It isn't until the window vanishes and the street seems to rush up at me that I realize I've jumped.

I wake up with the dawn, my head throbbing with the remnants of a pummeling dream. Behind the door, a key jangles in the lock.

Helen!

My headache vanishes. I jump up and strip down to my briefs almost without thought, as my penis is programmed to present a Welcome Home banging as soon as she crosses the threshold. It's all I can manage to refrain from pulling at myself as I walk.

I throw the door open. Manhaus looks down at my package. "Well, I'm happy to see you, too."

My penis wilts.

Manhaus fishes for something in his coat pocket. "Care for a smoke?"

I cannot speak.

He lights a cigarette. "I think you already know why I'm here. I told you long ago that house and man shall never touch. It's a cardinal rule, and fantasizing alone is sinful."

My lips move, but it doesn't feel like I'm moving them. "How—but—why—"

"That thing the foreman put on you does more than just explode, you know. It sends back all manner of data. Your lover was correct in saying the whole exploding-if-you-take-it-off bit was a bluff, but the data part, well, she couldn't know that, 'cause it's top secret." Manhaus rolls his cigarette from one side of his mouth to the other. "But I hate standing while I speak. Do you mind if I take a seat? Oh, and while I get comfortable, might you fetch me something to drink? Alcohol, if available."

Suddenly, I'm in the kitchen, pouring a drink. I have no memory of leaving Manhaus. Everything is wrapped up in cotton, and my heart beats in my ears. Most of the booze spills onto the counter, but only half my brain notices this. The other half is thinking about Helen.

Oh my god, what's he done with Helen!

141

But I can't let that part of my brain reach the forefront, because, if I do, all the walls in my brain house will crumble to dust.

Something flashes, and I'm in the living room, presenting the glass to Manhaus with a hand that doesn't feel like my own. Looking down with eyes that seem equally foreign, I finally see what was behind his back. An oversized cooler now rests by his feet.

"Take a seat."

My body moves to the sofa on the other side of the room.

"No, beside me."

My body obeys.

He downs the booze and picks up the cooler. He sits it on his lap and taps his fingers on the lid, fingers that now look like long, black carpentry (coffin?) nails.

"Sometimes, I get the feeling you still don't believe how serious we are, not even after you watched your friend turn into a pile of bricks." His fingers drum harder against the cooler. "Perhaps two demonstrations will convince you. I really hope so because it pains me to hurt you. I'm here to bring order, you see, not pain. Alas, it must be administered at times, and one of those times is now."

He empties the cooler; horror spills out onto the floor.

"Take a look at your lover. Still want to fuck her?"

Helen has been decapitated with a rough-hewn knife that protrudes from her neck stump. House maggots churn through puppet flesh.

"Guess you could stick your cock in her mouth and thrust around a bit, if you want. Laws don't apply to deceased houses, nor do they apply to me." Manhaus laughs. "I could lay you out on the floor now and fuck your brain out without incurring liability. It'd be fun, sure, but I'm in no mood to try your filthy kind."

I projectile vomit, and the muck strikes her face, sticking to it. I want to die.

"See your slut all covered in puke? Fitting for a *fazlir*—a miscegenating whore."

I don't hear Manhaus after this. Everything is red and green and purple and black and blue and discombobulated and swirling. The colors become fountains of madness, spurting up from hell. In them, I rip off my clothes and bathe, bathe myself in acid until my flesh melts and my skeleton runs away, cackling into the not-good-but-bad-oh-so-very-bad night. Inky blackness encases and becomes me.

Yes, I am blackness now; I am nothing; I am anti-matter; I am void.

CHAPTER ELEVEN

When I come to, I'm on the floor, and Manhaus stands over me, looking a hundred feet tall.

"Feeling better? You seem to have blacked out for a while there."

I don't feel better. In fact, I feel the closest to dead I've ever felt. I turn from him and see I'm back in the foreman's office in the factory. Somebody obviously undressed me, too. I'm clad in overalls.

Helen's head sits on the floor a few feet away, placed over a towel so as not to muck up the tiles. I stare into the empty eyes that I'd loved, hoping to once again find within them that special something she alone possessed, but they are vacant and will be eaten away by worms soon enough.

Something cracks inside, and I realize it's my humanity.

Manhaus taps his fists against her scalp as though knocking on a door. "But don't let this give you any ideas. Only a house soul can extinguish another house soul."

I want my voice to rise—to roar—but it exits as a wheeze. "She was the only thing I loved in this world."

Manhaus lifts me from the floor. His arm snakes across my shoulders, making me feel cold. "I know how you felt. I read the biometric data, remember? But because I'm the sentimental

sort, I'm going to do something for you that will help bring closure."
He snuffs out his first cigarette and lights another. "You can sleep
with her rotted head tonight."

The foreman forces me into bed. He has to strap me down.

Death is with me under the covers, reeking. I scream for
hours. My fellow workers can't sleep, and I don't care. Eventually,
I lose consciousness, but awake when a liquid stream splashes
against my chest. One of my roommates has his cock out and is
pissing on my lady's severed head, mocking her, calling her *a
fucking house bitch.*

I want to shatter my bonds, rise up, and piss on this man
like he pisses on Helen—preferably after I've killed him—but
something breaks inside me, something that's been cracking since
I first saw Helen dead, and, no matter how hard I try, I can't find
the shattered pieces.

The man returns to his bed when he's done pissing. He
goes off to sleep, but I never sleep again.

In time, rage dissipates along with my other emotions. Nothing
matters anymore—not even myself—so I let everything slide away
without fanfare. Attempts to maintain and hold onto *me* have
proven foolish; I'm sick of playing the fool.

I transform into a working machine, only breathing because
it maintains my inner gears and springs. If I fail to suck air, I won't
be able to pull the lever and open the mouth of the kiln, and that'll
never do. It no longer matters that I help compress the bodies of
my kind into bricks. It's okay. It's value-neutral. I'm only doing
what needs to be done.

At some point in the past—could have been yesterday or

500 years ago—one of my co-workers, an older man who probably should have been retired long before, fell down and broke his ankle. The supervisor came by a few minutes later and hustled him into a room whose door I never saw open unless two walked in and one walked out.

I just kept working, generally okay with the situation.

Shit happens.

And shit continues to happen, but it concerns me less and less until I notice nothing outside myself. The lever is a part of me, totally indistinguishable from flesh. When others sleep, I pull. The foreman likes my performance. I'm his best employee, but, in truth, I don't give a royal rat's ass what he thinks. A lever thinks and cares about nothing, you see. It just opens a door, closes it, opens it again.

I want to be more like a lever. That's all I think about.

And so—with a little time and practice—a lever is what I become.

A hand grasps my shoulder, but I don't jump. Steel never jumps.

Some house guy is flapping his lips at me. This is confusing. One isn't supposed to talk to a lever. One is supposed to pull it. Then I remember that a lever shouldn't ever be confused, but here I am, being confused.

I?

Suddenly, I remember: my name is Carlos and I'm human. This is an upsetting revelation. "What the hell do you want," I grumble.

Manhaus looks grave. "Your time has come."

"Really?" I return to pulling the lever, eager to bond with it again. "Well, Tippycanoe and Tyler, too."

Manhaus' hand falls on mine. "This factory last operated two days ago, but we decided to let you go at it for a little while longer. You seemed to enjoy yourself so much."

I look around. Apart from Manhaus and me, the factory is empty. "How old am I anyway?"

"505 human years."

I note my hands. Before, I hadn't realized how gray and withered they'd become. "Oh."

"You've done much in your time. Or majestic Heaven is almost complete, but we need to finish one last building—and your body will provide more than enough bricks for the job. This factory will shut down as soon as we create them, and the earth will fold it into its bosom until needed again."

"Shit, what am I going to do now?"

"That's what I want to talk to you about. You've been an excellent worker—dare I say you've gone above and beyond the call of duty—so I want you to serve as our capstone. The other surviving workers will die and rot away, but I'm giving you the opportunity to become a memorable and historic part of our Heaven. It's an honor, you know."

"Yep, guess it is"

"So you agree to this?"

"Whatever floats your boat, captain."

"Wonderful, but before we get going, there's someone here who wants to talk with you. I think you'll be interested in seeing her again."

"*Her*? *Again*?"

"Yes."

A few seconds of confusion, then I identify this strange new sensation inside me: *hope*. Could he be referring to my lady, back from the dead and restored to her former self? Hope collapses as a female house walks through the door, dressed in black leather and fishnets and painted up like a whore.

"This is your childhood home, Ruth," Manhaus says. "In the past, there was bad blood between you, but she is here today to put that aside and see you off."

She looks up at Manhaus. "Do I have to do this?"

He grabs her arm roughly. "You know the drill. Just say what I told you to say and be done with it!"

"Okay, okay, just let me go! God, I fucking hate retirement parties!" Once her arm is free she pauses to apply scarlet lipstick. Only after surveying the new coat in a pocket mirror does she continue: "I forgive you and your family for the things you did inside of me and for making me what I am today. Now I gotta leave, if that's alright with you." She bats her lashes at Manhaus, having never once made eye contact with me. "I'm late for a paid date."

I watch disinterestedly as the house in which I'd spent my formative years walks away, leaving the factory quickly and without a backwards glance.

"That went well, don't you think?"

"Sure did."

Manhaus fishes something out of his pocket. "And, before I forget, I'd like to present you with this pocket watch in honor of 475 years of constant and committed service. We engraved your name, but spelt it wrong. And you might have to tap the watch a bit to keep it going."

"Why bother?"

Manhaus slaps my back. "I like your new attitude. Too bad I didn't see more of it in the past. Oh well; what's done is done. In the end, I guess I'm somewhat grateful to you. You've done a lot in helping us build our city"—his eyes now look misty—"you stupid, stupid fuck."

"Right back at yah, chief."

He exhales deeply. "Then are you ready to take that walk?"

"As ready and raring as I'll ever be."

"Accompany me please to the retirement room. Someone awaits you there."

And so I follow him, without thought and without feeling.

"See you on the other side!" Manhaus then leaves me by the entrance.

"Whatever," I reply, and step through a door that slams shut behind me.

SECTION 3:

BRICK FOR BRICK

My experience as a brick began when my auxiliary system was activated by the touch of a worker's hand beneath a towel. I was given the customary pre-recorded message to say, only to be activated once, and not to be transmitted aloud but beamed directly into the skull of whatever worker caught me out of the kiln:

"*You will enjoy working with me. Just be sure not to place me against another brick before my time, or you will fucking pay.*"

Once he touched me, I was inside him. I know this only because I can access a record of the upload, and but cannot open the file itself as it's marked *unreadable*. I felt no side effects, or anything else, thereafter, though I'm sure I haunted this man—who I assume must now be a brick, too—and he translated my presence into images of skeleton fingers and feet.

It makes me sad, knowing I've haunted others as they've haunted me, but oh well...

I came into brickhood within the kiln, but it wasn't until all my pieces were brought together and connected to a larger structure of human bricks that I got past what had been scripted into me and began, in a sense, to *feel*.

Now, I experience myself not as flesh and bone but as a series of thirty-five bricks placed atop a high-price downtown condominium. There, I observe the family living directly below me. My new eyes-that-aren't-eyes are superior to my man-eyes, able to focus on house bodies and condense them so they appear less luminous and more human in shape.

I never like what I see: The husband—fat and lazy—is having an affair. His wife is too indifferent to notice, and the children do little more than watch TV and smoke the house equivalent of weed, though they no longer chip or draw on my walls, which is a relief.

I hope they move before I decide to collapse their ugly and complacent world down around them. At the moment, it's only my ability to observe a second family that stays my bricks. This other unit also has a dark and syrupy feel—like something invisible has exploded on the walls and rotted for days—but that's because the housemother there is old, decrepit, and lost within herself. Her adult daughter provides care, which lightens the atmosphere somewhat and, most of all, proves to me that not all houses are evil or indifferent assholes.

Realizing this makes me feel guilty for the things I'd imagined over and over again in my head-that-isn't-a-head, but, though I have no way of proving it, I'm sure I'm not the first human brick to have fantasies of smothering house babies and raping house women.

On bad days, when the dark muckiness *really* gets to me, and when not even the TV can provide sufficient distraction, I try to project my essence from the bricks, imagining it as a horrible, shambling corpse that the house family will see and tremble at. For the most part, they totally ignore or walk through it. At times, however, my efforts are seen, but it's usually not by the family but by some skittish house-aunt who's over for a visit. She probably thinks I'm the boogeyman from whatever house religion she subscribes to, and I get no satisfaction from that. I want everyone to know who and what I am.

Maybe, some day, I'll hold human form again. If I do, I'll treat my house with utmost respect; I won't allow black greasiness to set in. But how will I remember it's me if my body and face aren't the same? Even my old appearance is now difficult to recall. I remember that I once had a long nose and ears that were barely asymmetrical. I had dark blonde hair, pinkish skin, and slender fingers. I had boxers with lobsters and palm fronds printed on them, and I lived in a house that had a name. Maybe it started with an H, maybe an R. Then I wonder if I've ever been human, and if moving and talking weren't just things I dreamt about. I like to think that I'd been; that I did have a body at some point, and that I'm really not a thinking brick with identity issues that exists in the hereafter with a bunch of bug-fuck crazy house souls.

But I guess it's entirely possible that the opposite is true.

ABOUT THE AUTHOR

Kevin L. Donihe, perhaps the world's oldest living wombat, resides in the hills of Tennessee. He has published four other books via Eraserhead Press. His short fiction and poetry has appeared in The Mammoth Book of Legal Thrillers, Flesh and Blood, ChiZine, The Cafe Irreal, Poe's Progeny, Book of Dark Wisdom, Dark Discoveries, Bathtub Gin, Not One of Us, Dreams and Nightmares, Electric Velocipede, Star*Line, Sick: An Anthology of Illness, and other venues. He also edits the Bare Bone anthology series for Raw Dog Screaming Press, from which a story was reprinted in The Mammoth Book of Best New Horror 13.

Visit him online at myspace.com/kevindonihe

Bizarro books

CATALOGUE – SPRING 2008

Bizarro Books publishes under the following imprints:

www.rawdogscreamingpress.com

www.eraserheadpress.com

www.afterbirthbooks.com

www.swallowdownpress.com

For all your Bizarro needs visit:

WWW.BIZARROCENTRAL.COM

Introduce yourselves to the bizarro genre and all of its authors with the *Bizarro Starter Kit* series. Each volume features short novels and short stories by ten of the leading bizarro authors, designed to give you a perfect sampling of the genre for only $5 plus shipping.

BB-0X1
"The Bizarro Starter Kit"
(Orange)

Featuring D. Harlan Wilson, Carlton Mellick III, Jeremy Robert Johnson, Kevin L Donihe, Gina Ranalli, Andre Duza, Vincent W. Sakowski, Steve Beard, John Edward Lawson, and Bruce Taylor.

236 pages $5

BB-0X2
"The Bizarro Starter Kit"
(Blue)

Featuring Ray Fracalossy, Jeremy C. Shipp, Jordan Krall, Mykle Hansen, Andersen Prunty, Eckhard Gerdes, Bradley Sands, Steve Aylett, Christian TeBordo, and Tony Rauch.

244 pages $5

  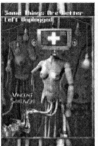 

BB-001 **"The Kafka Effekt"** D. Harlan Wilson - A collection of forty-four irreal short stories loosely written in the vein of Franz Kafka, with more than a pinch of William S. Burroughs sprinkled on top. **211 pages $14**

BB-002 **"Satan Burger"** Carlton Mellick III - The cult novel that put Carlton Mellick III on the map ... Six punks get jobs at a fast food restaurant owned by the devil in a city violently overpopulated by surreal alien cultures. **236 pages $14**

BB-003 **"Some Things Are Better Left Unplugged"** Vincent Sakwoski - Join The Man and his Nemesis, the obese tabby, for a nightmare roller coaster ride into this postmodern fantasy. **152 pages $10**

BB-004 **"Shall We Gather At the Garden?"** Kevin L Donihe - Donihe's Debut novel. Midgets take over the world, The Church of Lionel Richie vs. The Church of the Byrds, plant porn and more! **244 pages $14**

BB-005 **"Razor Wire Pubic Hair"** Carlton Mellick III - A genderless humandildo is purchased by a razor dominatrix and brought into her nightmarish world of bizarre sex and mutilation. **176 pages $11**

BB-006 **"Stranger on the Loose"** D. Harlan Wilson - The fiction of Wilson's 2nd collection is planted in the soil of normalcy, but what grows out of that soil is a dark, witty, otherworldly jungle... **228 pages $14**

BB-007 **"The Baby Jesus Butt Plug"** Carlton Mellick III - Using clones of the Baby Jesus for anal sex will be the hip sex fetish of the future. **92 pages $10**

BB-008 **"Fishyfleshed"** Carlton Mellick III - The world of the past is an illogical flatland lacking in dimension and color, a sick-scape of crispy squid people wandering the desert for no apparent reason. **260 pages $14**

BB-009 "Dead Bitch Army" Andre Duza - Step into a world filled with racist teenagers, cannibals, 100 warped Uncle Sams, automobiles with razor-sharp teeth, living graffiti, and a pissed-off zombie bitch out for revenge. **344 pages $16**

BB-010 "The Menstruating Mall" Carlton Mellick III *"The Breakfast Club* meets *Chopping Mall* as directed by David Lynch." - Brian Keene **212 pages $12**

BB-011 "Angel Dust Apocalypse" Jeremy Robert Johnson - Meth-heads, manmade monsters, and murderous Neo-Nazis. "Seriously amazing short stories..." - Chuck Palahniuk, author of *Fight Club* **184 pages $11**

BB-012 "Ocean of Lard" Kevin L Donihe / Carlton Mellick III - A parody of those old Choose Your Own Adventure kid's books about some very odd pirates sailing on a sea made of animal fat. **176 pages $12**

   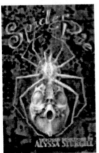

BB-013 "Last Burn in Hell" John Edward Lawson - From his lurid angst-affair with a lesbian music diva to his ascendance as unlikely pop icon the one constant for Kenrick Brimley, official state prison gigolo, is he's got no clue what he's doing. **172 pages $14**

BB-014 "Tangerinephant" Kevin Dole 2 - TV-obsessed aliens have abducted Michael Tangerinephant in this bizarro combination of science fiction, satire, and surrealism. **164 pages $11**

BB-015 "Foop!" Chris Genoa - Strange happenings are going on at Dactyl, Inc, the world's first and only time travel tourism company.
"A surreal pie in the face!" - Christopher Moore **300 pages $14**

BB-016 "Spider Pie" Alyssa Sturgill - A one-way trip down a rabbit hole inhabited by sexual deviants and friendly monsters, fairytale beginnings and hideous endings. **104 pages $11**

BB-017 "The Unauthorized Woman" Efrem Emerson - Enter the world of the inner freak, a landscape populated by the pre-dead and morticioners, by cockroaches and 300-lb robots. **104 pages $11**

BB-018   "Fugue XXIX" Forrest Aguirre - Tales from the fringe of speculative literary fiction where innovative minds dream up the future's uncharted territories while mining forgotten treasures of the past. **220 pages $16**

BB-019 "Pocket Full of Loose Razorblades" John Edward Lawson - A collection of dark bizarro stories. From a giant rectum to a foot-fungus factory to a girl with a biforked tongue. **190 pages $13**

BB-020 "Punk Land"   Carlton Mellick III - In the punk version of Heaven, the anarchist utopia is threatened by corporate fascism and only Goblin, Mortician's sperm, and a blue-mohawked female assassin named Shark Girl can stop them. **284 pages $15**

BB-021"Pseudo-City" D. Harlan Wilson - Pseudo-City exposes what waits in the bathroom stall, under the manhole cover and in the corporate boardroom, all in a way that can only be described as mind-bogglingly irreal. **220 pages $16**

BB-022   "Kafka's Uncle and Other Strange Tales" Bruce Taylor - Anslenot and his giant tarantula (tormentor? fri-end?) wander a desecrated world in this novel and collection of stories from Mr. Magic Realism Himself.   **348 pages $17**

BB-023 "Sex and Death In Television Town" Carlton Mellick III - In the old west, a gang of hermaphrodite gunslingers take refuge from a demon plague in Telos: a town where its citizens have televisions instead of heads.   **184 pages $12**

BB-024 "It Came From Below The Belt" Bradley Sands - What can Grover Goldstein do when his severed, sentient penis forces him to return to high school and help it win the presidential election? **204 pages $13**

BB-025 "Sick: An Anthology of Illness" John Lawson, editor - These Sick stories are horrendous and hilarious dissections of creative minds on the scalpel's edge. **296 pages $16**

BB-026 "Tempting Disaster" John Lawson, editor - A shocking and alluring anthology from the fringe that examines our culture's obsession with taboos. **260 pages $16**

BB-027 "Siren Promised" Jeremy Robert Johnson - Nominated for the Bram Stoker Award. A potent mix of bad drugs, bad dreams, brutal bad guys, and surreal/incredible art by Alan M. Clark. **190 pages $13**

BB-028 "Chemical Gardens" Gina Ranalli - Ro and punk band *Green is the Enemy* find Kreepkins, a surfer-dude warlock, a vengeful demon, and a Metal Priestess in their way as they try to escape an underground nightmare. **188 pages $13**

BB-029 "Jesus Freaks" Andre Duza For God so loved the world that he gave his only two begotten sons... and a few million zombies. **400 pages $16**

BB-030 "Grape City" Kevin L. Donihe - More Donihe-style comedic bizarro about a demon named Charles who is forced to work a minimum wage job on Earth after Hell goes out of business. **108 pages $10**

BB-031 "Sea of the Patchwork Cats" Carlton Mellick III - A quiet dreamlike tale set in the ashes of the human race. For Mellick enthusiasts who also adore *The Twilight Zone*. **112 pages $10**

BB-032 "Extinction Journals" Jeremy Robert Johnson - An uncanny voyage across a newly nuclear America where one man must confront the problems associated with loneliness, insane dieties, radiation, love, and an ever-evolving cockroach suit with a mind of its own. **104 pages $10**

BB-033 "Meat Puppet Cabaret" Steve Beard At last! The secret connection between Jack the Ripper and Princess Diana's death revealed! **240 pages $16 / $30**

BB-034 "The Greatest Fucking Moment in Sports" Kevin L. Donihe - In the tradition of the surreal anti-sitcom *Get A Life* comes a tale of triumph and agape love from the master of comedic bizarro. **108 pages $10**

BB-035 "The Troublesome Amputee" John Edward Lawson - Disturbing verse from a man who truly believes nothing is sacred and intends to prove it. **104 pages $9**

BB-036 "Deity" Vic Mudd God (who doesn't like to be called "God") comes down to a typical, suburban, Ohio family for a little vacation—but it doesn't turn out to be as relaxing as He had hoped it would be... **168 pages $12**

BB-037 "The Haunted Vagina" Carlton Mellick III - It's difficult to love a woman whose vagina is a gateway to the world of the dead. **132 pages $10**

BB-038 "Tales from the Vinegar Wasteland" Ray Fracalossy - Witness: a man is slowly losing his face, a neighbor who periodically screams out for no apparent reason, and a house with a room that doesn't actually exist. **240 pages $14**

BB-039 "Suicide Girls in the Afterlife" Gina Ranalli - After Pogue commits suicide, she unexpectedly finds herself an unwilling "guest" at a hotel in the Afterlife, where she meets a group of bizarre characters, including a goth Satan, a hippie Jesus, and an alien-human hybrid. **100 pages $9**

BB-040 "And Your Point Is?" Steve Aylett - In this follow-up to LINT multiple authors provide critical commentary and essays about Jeff Lint's mind-bending literature. **104 pages $11**

BB-041 **"Not Quite One of the Boys"** Vincent Sakowski -While drug-dealer Maxi drinks with Dante in purgatory, God and Satan play a little tri-level chess and do a little bargaining over his business partner, Vinnie, who is still left on earth. **220 pages $14**

BB-042 **"Teeth and Tongue Landscape"** Carlton Mellick III - On a planet made out of meat, a socially-obsessive monophobic man tries to find his place amongst the strange creatures and communities that he comes across. **110 pages $10**

BB-043 **"War Slut"** Carlton Mellick III - Part "1984," part "Waiting for Godot," and part action horror video game adaptation of John Carpenter's "The Thing." **116 pages $10**

BB-044 **"All Encompassing Trip"** Nicole Del Sesto -In a world where coffee is no longer available, the only television shows are reality TV re-runs, and the animals are talking back, Nikki, Amber and a singing Coyote in a do-rag are out to restore the light **308 pages $15**

BB-045 **"Dr. Identity"** D. Harlan Wilson - Follow the Dystopian Duo on a killing spree of epic proportions through the irreal postcapitalist city of Bliptown where time ticks sideways, artificial Bug-Eyed Monsters punish citizens for consumer-capitalist lethargy, and ultraviolence is as essential as a daily multivitamin. **208 pages $15**

BB-046 **"The Million-Year Centipede"** Eckhard Gerdes -Wakelin, frontman for 'The Hinge,' wrote a poem so prophetic that to ignore it dooms a person to drown in blood. **130 pages $12**

BB-047 **"Sausagey Santa"** Carlton Mellick III - A bizarro Christmas tale featuring Santa as a piratey mutant with a body made of sausages. **124 pages $10**

BB-048 **"Misadventures in a Thumbnail Universe"** Vincent Sakowski - Dive deep into the surreal and satirical realms of neo-classical Blender Fiction, filled with television shoes and flesh-filled skies. **120 pages $10**

BB-041 "Not Quite One of the Boys" Vincent Sakowski -While drug-dealer Maxi drinks with Dante in purgatory, God and Satan play a little tri-level chess and do a little bargaining over his business partner, Vinnie, who is still left on earth. **220 pages $14**

BB-042 "Teeth and Tongue Landscape" Carlton Mellick III - On a planet made out of meat, a socially-obsessive monophobic man tries to find his place amongst the strange creatures and communities that he comes across. **110 pages $10**

BB-043 "War Slut" Carlton Mellick III - Part "1984," part "Waiting for Godot," and part action horror video game adaptation of John Carpenter's "The Thing." **116 pages $10**

BB-044 "All Encompassing Trip" Nicole Del Sesto -In a world where coffee is no longer available, the only television shows are reality TV re-runs, and the animals are talking back, Nikki, Amber and a singing Coyote in a do-rag are out to restore the light **308 pages $15**

BB-045 "Dr. Identity" D. Harlan Wilson - Follow the Dystopian Duo on a killing spree of epic proportions through the irreal postcapitalist city of Bliptown where time ticks sideways, artificial Bug-Eyed Monsters punish citizens for consumer-capitalist lethargy, and ultraviolence is as essential as a daily multivitamin. **208 pages $15**

BB-046 "The Million-Year Centipede" Eckhard Gerdes -Wakelin, frontman for 'The Hinge,' wrote a poem so prophetic that to ignore it dooms a person to drown in blood. **130 pages $12**

BB-047 "Sausagey Santa" Carlton Mellick III - A bizarro Christmas tale featuring Santa as a piratey mutant with a body made of sausages. **124 pages $10**

BB-048 "Misadventures in a Thumbnail Universe" Vincent Sakowski - Dive deep into the surreal and satirical realms of neo-classical Blender Fiction, filled with television shoes and flesh-filled skies. **120 pages $10**

BB-049 "Vacation" Jeremy C. Shipp - Blueblood Bernard Johnson leaved his boring life behind to go on The Vacation, a year-long corporate sponsored odyssey. But instead of seeing the world, Bernard is captured by terrorists, becomes a key figure in secret drug wars, and, worse, doesn't once miss his secure American Dream. **160 pages $14**

BB-050 "Discouraging at Best" John Edward Lawson - A collection where the absurdity of the mundane expands exponentially creating a tidal wave that sweeps reason away. For those who enjoy satire, bizarro, or a good old-fashioned slap to the senses. **208 pages $15**

BB-051 "13 Thorns" Gina Ranalli - Thirteen tales of twisted, bizarro horror. **240 pages $13**

BB-052 "Better Ways of Being Dead" Christian TeBordo - In this class, the students have to keep one palm down on the table at all times, and listen to lectures about a panda who speaks Chinese. **216 pages $14**

 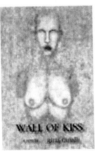  

BB-053 "Ballad of a Slow Poisoner" Andrew Goldfarb Millford Mutterwurst sat down on a Tuesday to take his afternoon tea, and made the unpleasant discovery that his elbows were becoming flatter. **128 pages $10**

BB-054 "Wall of Kiss" Gina Ranalli A woman... A wall... Sometimes love blooms in the strangest of places. **108 pages $9**

BB-055 "HELP! A Bear is Eating Me" Mykle Hansen The bizarro, heartwarming, magical tale of poor planning, hubris and severe blood loss... **150 pages $11**

BB-056 "Piecemeal June" Jordan Krall A man falls in love with a living sex doll, but with love comes danger when her creator comes after her with crab-squid assassins. **90 pages $9**

BB-057 **"Laredo"** Tony Rauch Dreamlike, surreal stories by Tony Rauch. **180 pages** **$12**

BB-058 **"The Overwhelming Urge"** Andersen Prunty A collection of bizarro tales by Andersen Prunty. **150 pages** **$11**

BB-059 **"Adolf in Wonderland"** Carlton Mellick III A dreamlike adventure that takes a young descendant of Adolf Hitler's design and sends him down the rabbit hole into a world of imperfection and disorder. **180 pages** **$11**

BB-060 **"Super Cell Anemia"** Duncan B. Barlow "Unrelentingly bizarre and mysterious, unsettling in all the right ways..." - Brian Evenson. **180 pages** **$12**

BB-061 **"Ultra Fuckers"** Carlton Mellick III Absurdist suburban horror about a couple who enter an upper middle class gated community but can't find their way out. **108 pages** **$9**

BB-062 **"House of Houses"** Kevin L. Donihe An odd man wants to marry his house. Unfortunately, all of the houses in the world collapse at the same time in the Great House Holocaust. Now he must travel to House Heaven to find his departed fiancee. **172 pages** **$11**

BB-063 **"Necro Sex Machine"** Andre Duza **400 pages** he The Dead Bicth returns in this follow-up to the bizarro zombie epic Dead Bitch Army. **$16**

BB-063 **"Squid Pulp Blues"** Jordan Krall **204 pages** In these three bizarro-noir novellas, the reader is thrown into a world of murderers, drugs made from squid parts, deformed gun-toting veterans, and a mischievous apocalyptic donkey. **$13**

COMING SOON

"Cocoon of Terror" by Jason Earls
"Jack and Mr. Grin" by Andersen Prunty
"Cybernetrix" by Carlton Mellick III
"Macho Poni" by Lotus Rose
"The Egg Man" by Carlton Mellick III
"Zerostrata" by Andersen Prunty
"Shark Hunting in Paradise Garden" by Cameron Pierce
"The Rampaging Fuckers of Everything on the Shitting
Planet of the Vomit Atmosphere" by Mykle Hansen

ORDER FORM

TITLES	QTY	PRICE	TOTAL

Please make checks and moneyorders payable to ROSE O'KEEFE / BIZARRO BOOKS in U.S. funds only. Please don't send bad checks! Allow 2-6 weeks for delivery. International orders may take longer. If you'd like to pay online via PAYPAL.COM, send payments to publisher@eraserheadpress.com.

SHIPPING: US ORDERS - $2 for the first book, $1 for each additional book. For priority shipping, add an additional $4. INT'L ORDERS - $5 for the first book, $3 for each additional book. Add an additional $5 per book for global priority shipping.

Send payment to:

BIZARRO BOOKS
C/O Rose O'Keefe
205 NE Bryant
Portland, OR 97211

Address	
City	State Zip
Email	Phone

Printed in the United States
105641LV00003B/184-204/P